MY
UNEXPECTED
LOVE

THE BEAUMONT SERIES - NEXT GENERATION

To all those who are seeking redemption

MY UNEXPECTED LOVE
HEIDI MCLAUGHLIN
© 2018

COVER DESIGN: Sarah Hansen: OkayCreations.
EDITING: Ellie: Love N. Books

ELLE

My head rests against the glass of the backseat window. Raindrops slide down, one meeting the other, forming a longer stream of water. Each one's only visible when we happen to pass under a streetlight. The edge of my fingernail follows the path until the small ball of water at the end meets the bottom of the window. I glance quickly at my phone, pressing the home button to bring it to life, only the solid black screen stares back at me.

It's dead, like how I feel on the inside.

"What time is it?" My voice is garbled and my breath poisoned by the harsh aftertaste of vodka, tequila, and whatever else I managed to get my hands on, causing my stomach to twist. Being underage hasn't stopped me from hitting every hotspot in Los Angeles, nor has it stopped the bouncers from letting me in. They all know who I am and not a single one of them cares because they know I'm there to spend money. Not to mention, I bring an entourage with me. For the club, it's free promotion considering every one of my friends details our outings on social media.

"Just after three." The driver's foreign accent makes it sound like he said tree or maybe it was free. My mind is mush, and I feel like I'm on the verge of passing out. I lift my head to glance at his GPS, only to have a wave of nausea roll through me. I press my forehead back to the cold window and close my eyes.

"How much longer?"

"We're here." The car comes to an abrupt stop, throwing my body forward. I look into the rearview mirror and meet the driver's eyes, and I swear he smirks. Blindly, I ruffle through my bag and pull out a twenty. The rate on the dash reads nineteen and some change.

"Here ya go." I toss the bill at him and exit the car. He screeches away within seconds of me closing the door. "Asshole," I mutter into the darkness.

Each step I take toward the apartment I share with my brother Quinn is painful. Tonight's outing is definitely one for the record books. Aside from the copious amounts of flowing alcohol, the all-night dancing has done a number on my muscles.

I don't know how long it takes with me fumbling around, trying to get my key in the lock before it opens. Quinn stands there, with his arm holding the door. The muscles in his arm strains, likely from the grip he has on the edge of the wood. The bright light from our living room lamp highlights his scowl almost perfectly, which is different for him because usually, Quinn's expressionless, always stoic. It's the troubled soul of a musician, only he's not troubled. I swear if he were, I don't think I'd be able to live with him.

"Thanks." I step in, brushing against him.

"We need to talk, Elle."

"Did someone die?" This is my automatic response to a statement like this. Quinn looks at me, his eyes cold and steady. I shrug. I know it's a bad joke, but whatever. I don't know why he expects anything different from me.

The door slams shut. The sound reverberates through the room, causing me to jump. "All right, can we at least turn the light off?" I shield my eyes when I look at him, exaggerating the fact that the light is too bright. His expression seems to worsen as he glares at me.

"Sit down." Quinn's command is forceful, demanding. He points to one of the two chairs we own. He's set them up across from one another in the middle of our living room, almost like an interrogation, or better yet an intervention.

"What's going on?" I sit with a huff, slouching in the chair with my legs kicked out in front of me. My brother sits down and grips the armrests, keeping his back straight and his eyes set on mine. Quinn is hard to read, always has been. I'm not joking when I say he's a tortured or troubled musician, even though he grew up in the lap of luxury. The stigma still applies to him. He's an old soul, according to our grandma, and carries some imaginary burden that only Quinn knows how to combat. "Quinn?"

"The partying has to stop, Elle."

"Excuse me?"

"I didn't stutter. For the past year, you've been out of control. Most nights, you don't even make it home. At first, I didn't think it was anything. Nothing out of the ordinary, since you're in college and this is what kids our age do, but recently, your habits are all over social media and Mom and Dad are throwing around words like court-ordered rehab."

My mouth suddenly dries, my stomach rolls and my temper is on the verge of exploding. No one, not Quinn, my parents or even my sister can understand what I've been going through. What Quinn couldn't bring himself to say is that since my twin sister almost died, since she was smashed up in a car, much like our father, and had to fight for her life, I haven't been right. Nothing in my life seems right anymore, and partying is the only way I know how to cope. The drinking allows me to stay numb, it keeps my mind in a fog, so I don't have to deal with the endless questions about how I'm doing, how Peyton is coming along or when am I going to settle down like her. The constant comparison, whether it's about our physical health or mental well-being is taking its toll. People seem to forget we're twins, but we're not the same person. "You have no right."

"I have every right. I'm tired of watching you self-destruct. I was there too, Elle. I almost lost my sister as well, but you don't see me drowning myself night after night with people who don't care about me, who won't protect me if something were to go wrong."

"No, you're perfect, right? You don't let anything affect you. You don't drink, do drugs or attempt to live life! You sit in your room, and write your songs, day after day and play them night after night at whatever bar or coffee shop will let you, until you get your big break. You sing to people who don't care about you, who won't rescue you if something were to go wrong. Seems we're not much different in the way we're coping."

Quinn shakes his head. "I'm not coping, Elle. I've moved on. I've come to terms with the fact Peyton almost died. It took me months, but you, it's... this has to stop. No one's saying you can't go out and have fun, but night after night drunken escapades have to come to an end. We are all in agreement, things have to change."

"Who's we?"

"Mom and Dad. Peyton and I. Ben."

"Ben?" My eyes divert to Quinn's, and he nods. I shake my head, wondering when my best friend decided to betray me. He's supposed to be my ride or die, but lately, he's been distant, standoffish. Maybe this is why. Could it be he's had enough of my crap and is trying to put some space between us? No, I don't believe it. If anything, he's got his nose in the books and is preparing for our upcoming finals.

"He's worried about you. We all are."

"None of you knows anything about me." My hands push into my hair as I grunt. I want to scream, to shove Quinn against the wall and yell until he finally understands what it's like to be me, if only for five minutes. Be Elle Powell-James, sister of Peyton who is engaged to Noah Westbury, and living their happy little life on social media for everyone to see. I shouldn't think this way when it comes to my sister because she's my lifeline, my best friend. There isn't anything I wouldn't do for her, and if she knew how I felt, she'd crumble. The last thing she would ever want to do is hurt me.

Quinn sighs and rubs his hands down the front of his legs. He's dressed like our dad, khaki shorts with combat boots with some random band shirt, likely a group from the seventies when 'music was real' and made with instruments and not computers.

"Dad received a call earlier tonight. He called me looking for you because your cell was going to voicemail."

"It's dead."

Quinn nods. "Anyway, I'm sure you know how your night went, but Mom and Dad received an eyeful when some journalists sent them pictures of you. I had to talk Dad into staying home, but he's angry, Elle."

"Well, his sister didn't almost die, did she?"

"At some point, Peyton's accident can no longer be your excuse. You used it to ditch out of a semester of school. You've used it for your grades and now this."

I turn away when I feel unshed tears threatening to escape. My throat tightens, and my body starts to ache. The impending onslaught of tears makes it hard to speak.

"These people you're hanging out with are making sure everyone knows everything about you. Every night they post videos of the person we love, falling down drunk, hanging on strange men, and almost passed out in random clubs, for our viewing pleasure."

"I haven't seen anything like that. How do I know you're not making this up?"

"Why would I? Why would I stay up until after three a.m. to have this talk with you if I were making any of this up? I value my sleep, Elle."

"My friends wouldn't do this."

"They're not your friends. They're leeches, using

you for your connections. They're using you for the star power, which comes with saying they've hung out with you. They don't care about you, no more than you care about them. How do you think Mom feels when she sees her daughter like that? Or Dad? Or the industry? You want to be a manager, but who's going to bring you on staff when they can Google you and see what your lifestyle is like. Like it or not, we're expected to act a certain way, behave as respected adults in the community. I don't think our parents are asking too much of us."

"And what if I don't want to, huh?" My tone is defiant and harsh.

"You don't have a choice."

"Says who?"

Quinn adjusts in the chair. He pulls out his phone, and by his movements, I'm guessing he's thumbing through his apps. He clears his throat. "Mr. and Mrs. James, We're writing to let you know our facility can accommodate Elle Powell-James when you see fit to admit her. Please note, this is an intense ninety-day treatment and visitors will not be allowed unless family counseling is needed. We will restrict all outside communications as well. We have a strict paparazzi rule, and our guards will ensure all photographers are kept off the property to protect Elle's privacy. Once you have your legal affairs in order, please let us know."

I swallow hard as I try to understand what Quinn is reading, and am unable to hold my tears at bay any longer. My parents aren't messing around, but what they don't understand is, I'm an adult, and I can make my own decisions. If I want to party, I can. If I want to drop out of school, I can. If I want...

"As you can see, Mom and Dad have had enough," Quinn interrupts my thoughts. "And I think you know this, which is why you've been ignoring their calls, not going home to see them and dodging their visits."

"I haven't—"

"You have. Before Peyton's accident, you and Mom spoke daily. When's the last time you spoke with her? When's the last time you've been home? If I had to guess, it was when Peyton was living there, but you haven't been back since."

"Texting is easier."

"Only because you can avoid the elephant in the room. You need help, Elle."

"I'm not going to some celebrity rehab center, Quinn."

"Then stop!" His voice echoes off the walls. "Grow up and start acting like someone who has a future instead of the Hollywood cliché."

"I'm not—"

"You are. That's what gets me the most, Elle. This person you've become is the same person you've mocked since you moved here. All our lives, you've said you'd never become the socialite who uses her name to get into clubs or restaurants, and now look at you. You've become the epitome of someone you despise."

"You don't understand."

Quinn nods. "I know, Elle. Peyton almost died. You're twins, you felt it. I've heard every excuse you can come up with, blaming whatever it is you have going on, on Peyton and the accident." He adjusts in the chair and leans forward with his arms resting on his legs. "Peyton's healed. She's moved on. She's planning a wedding, finishing college and trying to make peace with her life. If she can do it, then so can you." He taps my leg before getting up and leaving the room. I glance at the empty space Quinn's left behind. The bright light blinds me, causing me to turn away. As soon as I hear Quinn's door shut, I let the tears flow and the anger build. No one is going to tell me what to do with my life.

2

BEN

This is my usual spot. I'm sitting on the third to the last step of the concrete staircase, which leads to my apartment, waiting for Elle to come home. Night after night, I watch for the telltale sign of headlights and loud voices before I scurry up to my apartment, acting as if nothing is amiss. It's when I'm in my apartment; I become this peeping tom character who I loathe. It's not me, but the situation I'm in. Being in love with a woman who won't give me the time of day weighs heavily on my self-worth. I'm not being fair, though, and shouldn't assume Elle knows how I feel about her. It's not like I've come clean and put my feelings out there. I've kept them shriveled up at the bottom of my heart, mostly out of fear she'll reject me. I have no one to blame for my heartache other than myself.

After hours of sitting here, I'm numb. There are aches in parts of my body I didn't know existed, yet I stay Every person who uses the steps to reach the second and third floors stops and asks me if I'm okay. I am, truthfully, even if I want things to change. Elle worries me. Thoughts of her keep me up at night. I lose focus when I think about her, which is all the time, and yet this is the only way I can cope. I know I can go out with her, but being her standby, the guy who holds her coat at night and her hair when she's puking in the bushes isn't my idea of a good time. However, neither is this. Waiting here it's only increasing the anxiety I feel brewing inside. I don't want to see who she's coming home with, yet I know I'll look and let the pain of knowing some man is touching the woman I'm in love with flood through me.

At some point, you give up. Not emotionally, but physically, and you take your tired and sore legs up the stairs, one step at a time. And when you're inside your apartment, alone and in the dark, you start to ask yourself why. Why are you waiting for someone who doesn't wait for you? Why do you care? Why do you bother?

The answer is simple. I'm in love with her, and I have been since high school. For me, it was love at first sight. The love is unrequited, and for some reason, I'm okay with this because Elle is in my life, and having her there as a friend is better than the alternative.

I shut off all my lights and peek outside one more time before retreating to my room. I don't bother to change my clothes, and flop down on my bed. Deep down, I know I have to stop worrying about Elle, stop watching her self-destruct and trust her family will intervene. I'm Elle's best friend. I'll be her rock, her confidante and the person she unleashes her fury on after her brother tells her she needs help.

When he came to me with the plan, I surprised myself by agreeing with him. Usually, I have Elle's back, but in this case, he's right. She needs help. I don't know whether it's rehab or therapy, but she hasn't been right since Peyton's accident. I've tried to talk to her, but she changes the subject almost instantly, or she brushes it off with some good ole fun.

I startle at the sound of my phone ringing. It's her ringtone, a song designated just for her and one she chose for herself. I do not attempt to answer it, and instead, I stare at the dark ceiling, wondering what she has to tell me at three in the morning. My hand scrubs harshly over my face as the ringing starts again. I shouldn't answer it, but I know I'm going to. I always do even though lately I've felt like I've been nothing more than a stepping stone for her, a place for her to dump her problems. The door of friendship stops there. When it's my turn, she's busy, indisposed or doing who knows what and with whom. Peyton tells me this is a phase; her sister will snap out of it when Elle realizes she has feelings for me.

Peyton says I should ask Elle directly if she has feelings for me, but I'm afraid. I'm fearful of what she might tell me. To hear the words she's in love with someone who isn't me will be earth-shattering, and yet I've done nothing to prepare myself for it. My brother says I'm weak, and he's right, but love does that to a man.

However, she could tell me she's in love with me and expects to live a life of wedded bliss. I can't win with my heart and brain. It's an endless battle, and I have no one to blame but myself. Over the years, I've had ample opportunity to tell her how I feel, but the words have never come easy for me. Sure, I can say them in the mirror, behind her back when she's walking away, or after she's hung up, but to utter the words that will inevitably change our relationship to her face? I know it's something I will fail at.

The ringing stops, giving me a reprieve from the sound of the chime. I'm my own worst enemy when it comes to Elle, and yet I do nothing to change the situation. I suppose, in a way, I only have myself to blame for letting her get the best of me for so many years. I finally roll over and close my eyes, only to have her beautiful face appear and for her ringtone to fill my room once more.

"Let it go," I say into the darkness. "Let it go. Let it go. Let her go." The word *her* causes me to spring from my bed. I rub my hands over my face, pushing away the immediate sense of dread I feel before reaching for my phone. It starts ringing again and the picture of us that I took last week fills my screen. It's as if she knew I was about to call her. Only I don't accept her call right away. My mind is foggy and unsure. Why would I tell myself to let her go when I'm in love with her? I don't believe saying "let her go" was a slip of the tongue.

I finally roll over when the ringing continues. Elle's the only one who has no qualms about calling me in the middle of the night or this case, the wee hours of the morning. Given my earlier conversation with Quinn, I know why she's calling. I'm hesitant to pick up the phone, afraid of what she might say to me on the other end. With Elle, I can never be too sure.

Still, I press the button to open our line of communication because I'd hate myself if I didn't. "Are you hurt?"

"Yes."

"Pride doesn't count, Elle."

"You're supposed to have my back, Ben."

I brush my hand over my face and sigh. "I do, and I always will, but I happen to agree with your family. You've changed."

"Death does that to someone."

"No one died. Peyton is alive and well, and likely sitting in some class right now oblivious to your meltdown."

"That's rude."

"It's nearly four in the morning. I'm allowed to be a bit discourteous."

"Do you want me to let you go?"

Yes. "Never, Elle. You know I'll always be here for you."

"Why is life so hard, Ben?"

With no choice, I sit up and groan. My back presses into the hardwood of my headboard at an awkward angle. I quickly adjust, adding a pillow behind my back and get comfortable. "Life is what we make it, Elle. Right now, you're struggling emotionally, and the coping mechanisms you've chosen aren't healthy."

"You sound like Quinn. I want you to sound like Ben, my best friend."

I sigh. "I am your best friend, but I'm worried about you."

"Do you worry when you're with me?"

"I do, Elle. Every moment."

She sniffles and I want nothing more than to comfort her, but Quinn's right. We have to stand our ground and let her know she can't continue the way she is.

※

I NEVER THOUGHT I'd live in California, but here I am, following the girl of my dreams. I suppose it's not all bad considering my brother moved here shortly after I started at UCLA and had given me a place to escape my reality.

For the ten, eleventh or maybe it's the twelfth time I've yawned during class, garnering the attention of my professor. Admittedly, I'm not the only one who can't seem to stay awake during his lecture, but it seems I'm the one he's chosen to send death glares too. Had I known he would be here today instead of his assistant, I would've taken a sleeping aid or gone to bed early enough to be alert. The likelihood I would've done this is slim. I had to agonize over Elle all night, and I could've easily ignored her call, but the truth is, I never will.

She's my weakness.

My demise.

My professor moves to his podium signaling the end of his lecture and class. I start to gather my things as another yawn strikes. This time it's long and drawn out and as much as I try to hide it, my professor's eyes land on mine. Great.

"Mr. Miller, if you could please meet me in my office." He looks directly at me, so there's no mistaking it's me he wants to see, even though I look at the other students. Most are packing up their belongings, and only a few are looking at me. Their expressions tell me every-thing I need to know. I'm busted. For what, I don't know, but it seems I've done something to upset my teacher.

Like a child being scolded, I walk as slowly as possible down the hall of the building until I reach Professor Jacobs' door. I knock twice and wait for him to tell me to enter. His voice is loud as he beckons me in. My palms are sweaty, making it a bit tricky to turn the doorknob. It takes me a few tries before it finally opens.

I clear my throat when I enter. It's ridiculous because he already knows I'm here, but at least I'm not yawning. Being here makes me wonder if he wants to know whether his lecture was boring or if I'm not prepared for his class. Unfortunately, neither question has a positive answer.

"Mr. Miller, do you know why I called you here?" Clearly not, since I'm freaking out on the inside. If I did, I imagine I'd walk in with more confidence instead of preparing myself for a butt chewing.

"No, sir." Other than the fact I almost fell asleep in your class and had to fight to stay awake.

Jacobs slides a sheet of paper to the end of his desk and motions for me to take it. I do, waiting for the words to register in my mind. It's a letter addressed to me, from my dream agency in New York City. The agency I've always pictured working at, the one Elle used to tease me about because I would carry-on about their corporate information, studying and memorizing every bit.

"Dear Mr. Miller..." My words trail off as soon as my eyes land on the word internship.

"Do you want it? It's a great opportunity," Jacobs

asks. Inside, I'm screaming yes, but my head is shaking no. "Why not, Mr. Miller?"

My hand falls, but I refuse to let go of the paper. Why don't I want this opportunity to intern at the most prestigious advertising firm in New York? Elle. She's the reason. Yet, I can't find the words to tell my professor I'm going to turn this down because of a girl.

"Take some time to think about it."

"Thank you; I will." I turn and head toward his office door, stumbling my way through a mental fog. I'd be stupid to leave, but a complete fool to stay.

3

ELLE

*I*t doesn't matter how many times I look at the calendar, the dates aren't changing in my favor. I have four classes a week and three of my end of the quarter exams are on the same day. Some would say this is a twisted form of karma, but as far as I know, I haven't wronged anyone or the universe to deserve this sort of agony. Yet, here I sit with my study guides spread across the picnic table, watching my classmates as they do everything but study, wondering why I'm sitting here when I could be lounging under the shade tree or playing Frisbee with the guys from the baseball team. Surely, I can't be the only one who slacked off this quarter and is now in a mad rush to cram.

The truth of the matter is, I probably am, but honestly, no one has gone through what I have in the past year or so. I almost lost my sister, my twin no less. Something of that magnitude really screws with your psyche.

Quinn's right though, I'm not taking my life seriously. Thing is, I'm not sure I want to.

Life is supposed to be about living. Peyton's accident has shown me that. I don't want to spend countless hours combing through the material I'll likely never use again. I've seen the memes about any form of math ending in 'try" and can easily say the only one my profession will require is adding and subtracting, and the occasional percentage. Being a music manager has been my dream for as long as I can remember. The horrors my dad and uncles went through are things I never want my brother or any other musician to experience. This is the route my parents encouraged, but I think a well-placed internship might be a better angle for me. For one, there would no tests and no one telling me how to act. I'd be learning from the best and thrown into the mix right away instead of writing fifteen-page papers on how country music has shaped America, which in my mind is subjective.

However, I'm already facing academic probation and can't afford another screw-up. Since the other night when Quinn had a self-imposed intervention, I've done every-thing I can to avoid my parents. I was already giving them the cold shoulder, but now it's worse. For the most part, I've kept my phone off, turning it on only to see if Peyton or Ben has texted me, but even talking to Peyton right now is hard. She's harping on at me as well, but doing so in a sisterly fashion. I know she cares about me, she loves me, but enough is enough. My life is what it is right now, and I'm enjoying myself. As for my parents, I know my time is limited with them until one or either drive up and ream me a new one. I'm biding my time and failing grades this quarter will undoubtedly have my dad towering over me with his finger pointing in my face, screaming about how I'm throwing my life away, that I'm entitled and in need of help.

According to everyone except Peyton, I'm on a downward spiral, heading toward the bottom of the gutter, destined to piss my life away because I like to have fun and party. Quinn says there are unflattering pictures and videos of me online, but I've searched my friends' accounts and have come up empty. I wouldn't put it past my dad's publicist or legal team to make sure the pictures have been removed. He's always prided himself on keeping a squeaky clean image, and God forbid the less perfect of the twins do anything to tarnish his reputation.

A small breeze rolls over me, and I close my eyes, imagining it's my father. He's here, holding my hand, guiding me to make the right decisions. I don't remember him. I don't know his laugh or the way he would say my name. If it weren't for pictures and random home videos, I'd know nothing about my father other than what my mom or Uncle Liam have told me. My memories feel empty. There are times when I wish my father were still alive. Of course, it means I wouldn't have my dad and I'm not so sure I could live without him either. It's a hard line to tow, wanting both men in your life, but knowing if one is there, then the other could be hurting.

Chatter from my fellow classmates has me opening my eyes. They're hollering at each other, laughing and enjoying each other's company while I stress over the situation I've put myself in. It'd be so easy to quit. To throw my hands up in the air and say I'm done. In fact, the thought appeals to me. There would be no more early morning classes. I could do what I want and when. There would be no one to report to, telling me what to do or looking down on me because I messed up. I could start my own business. Sign some talent and get started on their careers. I know the ins and outs. I've been around the scene long enough to know how everything works. I have connections, a network built by the band from the many parties I've attended with them.

"That's what I'm going to do." As soon as I say the words aloud, the pressure I've been feeling starts to dissipate.

"What're you doing?" The voice behind me belongs to Quinn. I turn to find him standing there, looking every bit like our dad with his combat boots, baggy shorts, and the beanie... always with the beanie. The only thing missing is the tattoos. While our dad is covered, Quinn has opted to stay ink-free. If there were ever to be a movie about the band, Quinn would have the lead for Harrison James, drummer extraordinaire.

He doesn't wait for me to respond as he walks around the table and takes a seat opposite of me. I start to pick up my papers, and he helps. Stacking them nicely and handing me the small pile he's created.

"Thank you."

"You're welcome. You were gone before I woke up this morning. It's unlike you."

"Long day. Finals are coming up."

"Are you prepared?"

I shake my head and feel my throat tighten. As much as I want to be angry with him, I'm not. He means well, even if it's underhanded and a bit demeaning. I'm an adult and can take care of myself.

"Would you like me to help you study?"

"I think I'm going to drop out." The way Quinn's eyes widen, you would think I dropped a bomb on him. I suppose, in a sense, I have. "I'm behind, and my focus isn't on school."

"It's on the social scene."

"No, I'm focused on life and what I want to do."

"And what's that, Elle?"

I lean forward, almost as if I'm telling him the best-kept secret. "Music. It's my passion. My desire to make musicians like you feel appreciated in an industry which is hell-bent on destroying peoples' dreams."

Quinn looks around, turning his head from side to side. He does this often, especially before he's about to sing or when he wakes up. He says it's to loosen the muscles around his throat. I think it's a nervous tick, but who am I to argue.

"Let me get this straight." Quinn leans forward, bowing his head so only I can hear him. "You're planning on dropping out, days after I told you Mom and Dad aren't happy with you, to pursue a managerial role in music with no one currently signed under your company? Do I understand you correctly?"

I nod. I smile. My heart drops when I see Quinn's expression change from contempt to annoyance, maybe even anger.

"What?"

Quinn shakes his head and throws his hands up in the air. "What part of this makes sense to you, Elle? From day one, our parents have pushed our educations on us, making sure we had a backup plan. Pushing us to be better than them at everything we do so we'll never have to struggle."

"Are you serious right now? We have trust funds, Quinn."

"And you think the money will last forever?"

"No, but—"

"There are no buts, Elle. This is real life, and right now, I think you're a coward. You messed up, and instead of fixing it you want to quit. You want to throw in the towel and have a pity party for one."

"Two," I counter. "Ben will back me up."

"You don't get it."

"I do, Quinn. I'm supposed to be perfect like Peyton. I'm supposed to be this good little girl who never steps out of line."

"Peyton isn't perfect. Neither am I. No one has ever said we have to be perfect. Yes, our parents have expectations, but whose don't? You know what, don't answer that. I'm sure your friends' parents don't care what they're children do. Ours do, and I feel like I'm beating a dead horse."

"Well, stop."

He nods. His lips form a fine line. I know I've won this battle. "You're right, but since you're going to be a college dropout, I'm not comfortable with you taking on the role of my manager, so... yeah." My mouth opens as Quinn stands, avoiding all eye contact with me.

"You can't be serious?"

"I am, Elle. There's a reason you followed me here.

It's because of the education and what you're learning. Having a network already bodes well in your favor, but being business smart makes a manager more attractive in my opinion. I want someone who is going to protect me, and right now, you're a bit self-absorbed for my liking."

Quinn walks away before I have a chance to form a comeback. He's wrong on so many levels. I don't need a college education to be a good manager. My compassion should be enough. My love for music and knowledge of the scene should be the driving force behind any musicians or bands' desire to work with me. However, I was relying on Quinn to be my first client, to be my flagship star. Together, I expected us to move mountains.

Digging my cell phone out of my bag, I turn it on. As soon as it comes to life, messages roll in. Most of them are from my friends, or the people Quinn says are using me. One message catches my attention. It's from Peyton, asking me what I'm doing for Ben's birthday. Quickly, I go to my calendar because surely I haven't forgotten my best friend's birthday. The date, today, glares at me, mocking me for being so lost in my own world I've completely spaced off his most important day. I have to fix this because Ben deserves better.

I type my reply to Peyton: **Super short notice. Finals have me cray. Surprise party on Friday. Can you come?**

Yes. Noah says we'll be there. We'll stay at Mom and Dad's though.

Thank you! Party of the century!!

Oh, Ben will love this... not!

She's almost right. Ben will love having a birthday party, but it'll be low key and our close friends and family. I'll force Quinn to be there if I have to, but having Peyton and Noah come to town will make Ben's day. It's important to me he's happy. I know I don't always show him how much I care or what our friendship means, but he was my rock when Peyton had her accident. If it weren't for Ben, I don't know how I would've made it through the ordeal. There were countless nights I cried myself to sleep with his arms wrapped around me, holding me. His words were comforting, reassuring and hopeful. Ben is every bit my best friend, and I'd be lost without him.

4

BEN

*I*t's been my norm to stay on campus as long as possible after class. It's easier to study here, and I have unlimited access to the library. Plus it gives me the opportunity to be a college student. Something I've missed since I've lived off campus this entire time, and while I like where I live, the complex is noisy, and there are far too many distractions, Elle being the biggest one of all. She knows I'd drop everything for her, but she's also aware my grades are important to me. We've often joked about how our futures could align, with her in the music industry and me doing all her bands' marketing.

I suppose there's a chance those jokes or even dreams won't come true if I don't take the internship. I can put my dreams on hold and follow her around. It's what I've been doing since we graduated college. I never wanted to come to UCLA, but it's where she was going and the thought of not seeing her every day physically pained me. I know it's not normal to feel this way about someone, especially when I've been so clearly friend zoned, but I do. If asked, I'd move heaven and earth for her. I wish I could say she'd never ask, but the thing is, she would and likely will someday and with my current mindset, I'd do whatever I could to please her.

The letter Professor Jacobs handed me the other day sits on the table, most of it underneath my textbook. I can see the address of the firm, peeking out. It's one I memorized the day I figured out I wanted to work in advertising. To have the ability to create and engage an active audience through visual technique and words is fascinating. To learn from the best would be career defining. It's my dream, and yet I haven't told anyone about it. I wish I knew why.

I pull my book down, covering the rest of the paper. Right now, I'd rather not see it and feel like I'm making a rash decision. Everything I do or have done in the past, I've thought out fully or to the extent of Elle pleading with me. She means well, and I love her. Why wouldn't I follow her everywhere?

Thing is, she could come with me to New York when the quarter's over, assuming I have a job lined up. There are musicians in the bars there, she could easily find talent. We could share an apartment and go on pretending we're best friends and one isn't madly in love with the other.

"Yep, it'll never work," I mutter to myself, albeit a bit too loudly considering the amount of shushing going on in the library. I close my book and gather my papers before stuffing them into my bag. My last class is halfway across campus, and if I leave now, I can stop for something to eat and maybe a coffee. The extra dose of caffeine will do me some good and at least keep me from yawning in Jacobs' class. The last thing I need is to upset him and have him yank my recommendation away.

Somewhere on campus, Elle should be studying. I thought about finding her, but neither of us would get anything done. In high school, we tried being studious, but other things would get in the way. Her house was always loud, between her sister, brother or her dad and the band, it was a revolving door of fun, and I was happy to be a part of it all. Elle wasn't allowed at my house if my mother wasn't home, even though we broke this rule a few times. My mom never believed me when I would say Elle and I were friends, and the last thing she wanted was to be a young grandmother. While I can assure her I have no children, I'm not so sure my brother can say the same thing.

As soon as I walk into the coffee shop, my work-study co-workers shout, "Happy Birthday." With my coffee in one hand and a muffin in the other, I take the last available seat, next to the window and pull out my textbook. The pages are old, dog-eared, covered in highlighter and ripped in places, making it hard to read. This is what I get for living on a budget. I keep telling myself it'll all be worth it, especially with this internship. I know if I don't take it, I'll regret it. However, what happens if I do?

My life shouldn't be based on whether or not Elle is going to be there or not. Our friendship should withstand whatever career decisions we make. I'm not sure my heart will though. Color me a fool, chasing a girl who doesn't want to be caught.

The words on the page blur together. My mind is unfocused, and I feel as if I'm not prepared for this test. It's very unlike me to stress this much, but I want to pass it with flying colors, so Jacobs knows I'm serious about my future. I don't know what to do about New York, but I do know Jacobs is waiting for an answer. I close the book, finish my coffee and toss the rest of my muffin in the trash as I head to the door.

The late afternoon sun feels hotter now than it did earlier, but I still find myself looking at it, wondering what the sunset will look like tonight. I have to admit, the sunsets here during the summer are amazing. For what, I'm not sure. It's a reassuring feeling I get when I'm afforded the opportunity to watch.

I'm the first to arrive at Jacobs' class. Thankfully, he's nowhere to be seen, and if I have any sort of luck on my side, his grad assistant will be the one administering today's test. I use the few minutes of quiet to close my eyes. I'm exhausted. Sleeping in a strange bed hasn't done much for me, but going home would've been worse in my opinion.

I jolt awake at the sound of voices and quickly wipe at my chin, afraid I was drooling. Clearing my throat and sitting up, I smile at my classmates. A few give me strange looks, confirming I did, indeed, fall asleep. I can only hope I wasn't snoring.

Thankfully, Jacobs' assistant enters the room, giving me a reprieve for a few more hours. I'm not ready to give my professor an answer on the internship. I want to talk to Elle and see what she thinks. Her opinion is important to me, and I've always shared things with her.

The assistant starts the clock, and I get to work on what feels like a senior thesis more so than a test. Once again, I find myself out of focus and need to rub my eyes to clear away my blurred vision. When the graduate student announces we have ten minutes left, I feel as if I haven't written a single word, yet the page is covered in my messy handwriting. I barely have time to look over what I wrote when he calls time, and my classmates start to walk down the steps to drop off their papers. He doesn't say anything as I set mine in the basket, nor does he even look in my direction. Honestly, why should he? To him, I'm nothing more than a number.

On my way out of class, a few of the women smile and tell me they'll see me later. I shake my head and say nothing. I don't know if they're assuming I'll be at one of the many frat parties tonight or what, but the likelihood is, I won't. I want to head home, take a swim, relax in the hot tub and finish my night off with a long shower with decent water pressure. The rooms on campus lack greatly in this department.

The traffic home is light, and I'm there within twenty minutes. The sun has set, and I'm honestly surprised to find our outside pool empty since it's so warm out. A quick peek inside our rec room shows it's empty, which is perfect. I like the solitude, the peace, and quiet.

I walk past Elle and Quinn's door and pause. My hand's raised to knock, but I refrain. I'm not sure why, other than I need to decompress this evening. There's no doubt in my mind Elle will be over later or at least call me. A few hours by myself will be enough

After I unlock and open my door, I jump at the loud

chorus of voices yelling "surprise." In the center of my room stands Elle, she's wearing a party hat and blowing one of those ridiculous paper horns. Peyton and Quinn flank her, and while Noah's here as well, there's a group forming around him. I don't envy him for a second with his career. The poor guy can't go anywhere without someone asking for his autograph or a picture. Same goes for Quinn and his music. He already has a fan base following him around. I suppose they're all used to it though.

"Happy birthday," Elle says to me as she wraps her arms around my waist. This feels good, holding her close to my body. I'm not sure I can let her go for the last quarter of school.

"Thank you." I look into her blue eyes and know I can't leave. Tearing my gaze away from her, she uses this moment to disengage from me. The loss is immediately felt and is a stark reminder we're only friends. I look at the rest of the people in my small apartment and nod. "Thank you all for coming. This truly means the world to me."

One by one, people come up to me, shaking my hand and giving me well wishes. Most of these people I've never seen before in my life, and it makes me wonder who they are, where they came from and why they're here. Most, if not all, have to be friends of Elle's, which has me questioning, is this my party or hers?

There are a few classmates, and the girls who said they'd see me later are here. I can't remember their names though, and they didn't bother telling me what they are when they wish me a happy birthday. They're in the corner, chatting up Quinn, who raises his bottle of water in my direction. I wish I had his charm when it came to the opposite sex. If I did, I probably wouldn't pine after Elle the way I do.

"Hey, thanks for coming. You guys didn't have to fly in from Chicago for this." I kiss Peyton on her cheek and shake hands with Noah. Since Peyton's accident, she and I have grown closer. We've become each other's confidant, and she's really the only one who knows how I feel about Elle. For a while, we thought Elle was dating someone. I'm still not convinced she isn't, but whoever it may be, they never come around. I wouldn't put it past Elle to date someone her parents don't approve of either. Lately, she's on this rebellious streak, trying to make the most out of her life, according to her.

"We're happy to be here, Ben," Peyton says. "Besides, I miss my parents and the beach."

"And the warmer weather," Noah adds.

"Yeah, you guys had a major snowstorm the other day. I can easily say I'll take the L.A. weather over Chicago's."

"You're telling me. Thankfully, I don't have to shovel. I never thought I'd love living in an apartment, but let me tell you, it's heaven right now." Noah looks at Peyton with nothing but love in his eyes. I have no doubt this is exactly how I look at Elle. The only difference is Peyton returns his admiration, and Elle, well I'm not entirely sure because I refuse to ask, out of fear. I don't want her to tell me we're friends and we'll never be anything more. Deep down, I know this. I just don't need to hear the words.

5

ELLE

From where I stand, Ben and his brother are in deep conversation. Every so often, Brad looks around the room, probably eyeing up his next conquest or weeklong girlfriend. For as long as I've known him, he's never dated anyone past the seven-day mark. Back in high school, girls flocked to him. The appeal is there. He's the bad boy with a hot body and his always tousled hair, constant stubble, and lived-in leather jacket. When he turned seventeen, instead of cashing his savings in for a reliable car, he bought a motorcycle. I used to tease Quinn, saying Brad fit more into our family than he did.

I used to wonder when Ben was going to morph into Brad given that he used to idolize him when we were young, but, as we grew older the change never came. Ben was and still is my good guy. The one I can count on for anything. Peyton says I'm too dependent on Ben, and maybe she's right, but I can't imagine my life without him.

Brad nods to me and raises his beer in what I'm guessing to be a silent thank you for throwing his brother a birthday party. To this day, Brad still doesn't understand I would do anything for Ben.

"Elle, we should have been cutting the cake." Peyton's voice tears my gaze away from the Miller brothers.

"Otherwise I'm liable to bump into it, and I can't control what my hand does." I turn and look at my soon to be brother-in-law who shrugs.

"You wouldn't."

He nods and smiles brightly. "I would. I'm hungry."

"There's a ton of food here." I point over his shoulder where the six-foot-long table has everything from pizza, wings, chips, and dips to finger sandwiches.

"Ever since we went cake tasting, it's all he's been asking for." Peyton puts her arms around his waist and pulls him closer, resting her head on his chest.

"You went cake tasting without me?" There's a definite whine in my voice. Peyton picks her head up and looks away sheepishly. "P?"

"It's my fault," Noah says. "There was this bridal expo in town and a few weeks back, and we went."

"Without me? You didn't even tell me?"

"I didn't want you to stress with finals coming up, Elle. I promise." Peyton pulls away from Noah to take my free hand in hers. I down the rest of my wine before glancing at her. By the look in her eyes, she knows I'm upset. I don't really want to hurt my sister's feelings, but I want to be there when she plans her wedding. She's only dreamed of marrying Noah for as long as I can remember, and I want to help her make her fairy tales come true. "I haven't planned a single thing. Noah and I went to look, and truthfully, he had to force me to go."

"Kicking and screaming," Noah adds.

"Hey, are we going to cut the cake?" Quinn interrupts. Noah gives him a high-five while Peyton giggles and I roll my eyes.

"You too?"

Quinn shrugs. "What am I missing?"

"Nothing, come on." With my family behind me, we meander through the student body. Every few steps, someone tries to stop Noah and talk football. He's polite though and tells him he'll circle back around later. I don't know how he does it. If it's not people asking about his dad, they're on him about football. Growing up in Beaumont, no one really bothered with us, no one really cared. The band was always good to our community, and I think giving us the privacy we needed to grow up normal was their way of thanking them.

Quinn and Noah holler out to the room, asking them to quiet down for me. "Ben, if you could come over here for a second." Ben makes his way through the crowd. He's about six inches taller than most of the group, with the exception of Noah and a few other guys. "Everyone, on the count of three we're going to sing happy birthday to my best friend." I put my arm around his waist and look at him as I start to sing. For most of the song, he's staring at me. I can't ascertain what his expression means. He's not smiling, but not frowning either. Unfortunately, I'm not very good at reading people. I want to ask him what he's thinking, but the song is coming to an end, and his attention is no longer focused on me, but at the room full of his friends.

"Thank you. This has literally been the best surprise of my life. And thank you, Elle, for doing this."

"You're welcome. Now let's cut the cake."

"Yes, please!" Noah and Quinn yell out in unison. I turn away from Ben and hand him the knife, while Peyton starts pulling apart the paper plates. Once Ben slices through the cake, I take over and finish, making sure he gets the first piece.

"I know you didn't make this, but it's delicious. Thank you."

Again, I tell him he's welcome before he disappears into the crowd. Once everyone has cake, Peyton and I rest against the table, eating our slices, and watch as everyone mingles. "I'm going to see if Ben needs anything." I polish off another glass of wine. I promised myself I wouldn't drink, but I need the liquid courage to get through the night.

When I finally make it over to him, he's chatting up one of the girls from his class. I have no idea who she is, but she keeps putting her hand on his arm, and when she laughs, she throws her head back. Instantly, I'm not a fan. She's trying too hard.

"Hi, I'm Elle," I say, sticking my hand toward her.

"Bailey," she says as she reaches for my hand. Her handshake is weak and has no conviction, and her eyes shift back to Ben's instead of mine. I can tell she likes him. Ben and Bailey. Bailey and Ben. Nope. I don't like it. I step closer to Ben and hook my finger into his belt loop, pulling him closer to me. He leans toward me, smiling, as I move my finger over his upper lip.

"You have a bit of frosting here." He doesn't, but I want to send Bailey a message. My Ben needs someone like me to take care of him.

Ben's hand rests on my waist. He leans farther down, so his lips are close to my ear. "Are you drunk?"

I shake my head, hating myself because the lie comes easily. Tonight has to be about Ben and not my issues. The last thing I want is for him to worry about me. He needs to have fun and enjoy his birthday party. He can scold me later after everyone is gone.

"I think you are."

Instead of answering, I lean my head on his chest and start swaying to the music playing in the background. I don't know what song's playing, but I like it. It's slow and sensual, and I find myself pushing into Ben. His hand moves from my waist as his arm brings me even closer, pressing his body into mine. I don't know how long we stay like this, but with the combination of his arms around me, our bodies aligned and the beating of his heart against mine, I find myself crying.

My body shudders as a sob works its way through. "What's wrong?" he asks. The only response I can muster is to shake my head. Ben knows better though. He always does.

He pulls away and yells out that the party is over. A few people groan, and I use this time to slip into the bathroom to clean up. My reflection is nothing to be proud of with my black mascara leaving tear stains down my cheeks. "So much for waterproof." I take my sweet time, hoping everyone is gone when I emerge. Only Peyton and Noah are left. My sister rushes over to me and pulls me into her arms.

"Are you okay?"

"I'm fine, just had a moment." What the moment was, I have no idea. I don't know what came over me and or why my emotions are getting the best of me. "I'm going to stay and clean up."

"Do you want me to help?"

"No, go on. You and Noah have a long drive down to Mom and Dad's, and I'm sure you're both tired. I'll call you in the morning."

Peyton and I hug, and Noah comes over to kiss me on the forehead. As soon as I hear the door shut, I'm in the kitchen grabbing a garbage bag.

"What was that?" Ben asks, leaning his hip against the counter.

"What?"

He points over his shoulder and laughs. "Your overly possessive display of affection. Are you jealous of Bailey?"

"No." I step by him and start picking up every bottle and tin can I find.

"I think you are." Ben tosses a few into the bag.

"You're being ridiculous." The bottle of wine I opened earlier is still there. Sitting next to it is an empty one, which honestly I don't remember drinking. I pick it up, bringing the glass rim to my lips and drink the remaining contents, swaying a bit as I drop the bottle into the bag.

"You're drunk." Ben tries to take the bag from my hand, but I pull away.

"Am not."

"You are. I'm fairly certain you drank both bottles of wine."

"Peyton had some."

Ben shakes his head. "Peyton doesn't drink, and you know it."

"It's because she's so perfect right, is that it? Do you like her or something?"

"Elle..."

"No, don't 'Elle' me." I drop the bag and step toward him. He reaches out to catch me as I lose my balance. "You and Quinn are the same. Always harping at me about my drinking and throwing Peyton in my face and how perfect she is. Do you like her, Ben? I know you spent a lot of time with her at the hospital and when she was living with my parents. Did something happen between the two of you?"

He looks at me and frowns.

"Think long and hard about your answer because—"

"Because what? You'll be mad at me if I did something with Peyton?"

"You know what, I don't need this." I sidestep, only to have him grab my arm and pull me back to him.

"You don't get a say in who I like or what I do with other women, Elle."

"Let go of me, Ben." He does but keeps one hand on my waist.

"Your sister is in love with Noah."

"And you're in love with her!"

Ben shakes his head and steps away from me. He bends down for the bag and continues to pick up the empty bottles. "Go home, Elle."

"No, I told you I'd help. I made this mess, and I'll clean it up." I reach for the bag and try to tug it out of his hand. His resistance is causing the bag to sway back and forth, hitting us both in the legs. "Let go."

"No."

"You're such a child." I yank harder this time, and so does he, the thick plastic stretching.

"And you're drunk and in need of some help. Don't you see it? You're self-destructing, and there isn't anything we can do to stop you. I want to though. I want to be the friend you need, help you through whatever's going on in your head." Ben steps closer and points to his temple. "Let me help you, Elle."

"There's nothing wrong with me," I roar as I push him away. I'm angry and keep pushing until Ben's back is against the wall on the opposite side of his apartment.

"Elle?" His hand comes toward me, but I bat it away. He tries again, and this time I close my fist and cock my arm back. I try with all my might to hit him, but he's faster than I am. His hand closes around my fist, and the force of my movement has me crashing into him.

I look into his eyes as a barrage of hateful words form in my head. I expect Ben to let me go, but he doesn't. He places his arm around my back and pulls me to his body just as his lips press against mine.

6

BEN

For years, I've imagined what it would be like to kiss Elle, to finally feel her lips touch mine, to have her body pressed against me, and to have her fingers tug at the ends of my hair. I can easily say, without a doubt, that it's the best feeling in the world. In fact, it's more than that, because she's not pulling away. She's not pushing against me, telling me to stop, even though, deep down I know we should. However, for the life of me, I can't bring myself to be the one to suggest we take a step back because I want this. I've wanted to kiss her for as long as I can remember. For purely selfish reasons, I wrap my arm tightly around her in hopes of memorizing her and this moment.

Elle's fingers loosen their grip on my hair, leading me to believe this is over. It's fine. This will go down as one of the best birthday gifts of my life. I can live with this, burying it deep in my subconscious. Only her hands are now on my waist with one under my shirt. Her fingers are ice cold. They're a welcome reprieve against my scorched skin. Her other hand is tugging at the button on my jeans. Any moment now she's going to realize what's going on and step back, flushed not because we're making out but because she's embarrassed by the fact that it's me she's kissing, and I don't want to see her like that.

"Elle." My strangled and broken voice sounds nothing like me.

"Don't talk, Ben."

"We should stop." Even though I don't want to, Elle is who I picture my life with, the woman I see bearing my children, raising a family and growing old with. I've tried to see others in this role, but to no avail. It's always Elle.

"No, we shouldn't." Her lips are everywhere, while I stand here like a fish out of water looking for oxygen. I close my eyes and picture us together, between my sheets, moving fluidly against one another.

"You've had a lot to drink."

"I'm not drunk."

"I didn't say you were, but I want you to think about what you're doing, what we're about to do. Because there's no turning back, Elle."

"I want this, Ben."

That's all I need to know. I bend down and slide my arms under her legs. She reacts instantly, hopping into my hold and wrapping her legs around my waist. Hands are everywhere. Mine are firmly gripping her ass, and hers are cupping my face. Our lips fight for dominance over one another while I navigate toward the couch. There's nothing like a great make-out session to end the semester and the perfect birthday party.

"Bedroom," she says, tearing away from my mouth. Her lips press against the stubble on my jaw, until she reaches my ear. I suck in a deep breath when her teeth pull on my lobe, the sharp sting sending minute shock waves through my body. I must be dreaming. None of this can actually be my reality. With my luck, I'm going to wake up in the middle of my living room floor, naked as the day I was born, and suffering from a massive hangover.

Except, I know I didn't drink very much, especially when I'm around Elle out of fear she'll overdo it and I need to come to her rescue. We stumble into my wall, causing us both to disengage from each other. I use this time to ask the dreaded question. "Are you sure?"

Her response isn't verbal, but there's no way I can misinterpret what her hand means when it's pressing against my crotch. I fumble with my door, kicking it open once the knob turns. As many times as I've stumbled through my room, I've never tripped, until now. Thankfully, we land on my bed, both of us groaning and readjusting until she's scrambling away from me. I sit back on my knees, waiting for her to tell me what we're doing is a mistake, but she doesn't say anything.

"Elle?"

The only response I receive is the lifting of her shirt. I swallow hard at the sight of her body, one I've seen many times in a bikini, but this time everything is different. She reaches behind her, and I know she's unclasping her bra. That should really be something I do, but maybe she knows I'm nervous and is trying to show me she wants to be with me.

I follow suit and start undressing. Before I know it, we're both on our knees, facing each other, naked, and my God is she beautiful. Elle pushes her long dark hair over her shoulders, giving my eyes access to every part of her chest. For years, I could only dream about seeing her in the flesh, and now here she is.

"Touch me." Elle reaches for my hand, pulling me toward her until my hand is firmly cupping her breast. I'm at a loss for words, which I should be. My actions need to be loud and clear where she's concerned. I move forward. My free hand grips the back of her neck, bringing her closer. Our lips touch, tongues collide, and hands move freely against each other. She's on top, grinding into me, and then it's me pressing into her before I can no longer stand not knowing how she feels.

I pull the drawer of my bedside table open. In the process, I knock over an uncapped bottle of water, the contents gushing out onto the floor. Normally, I'd be upset and rush to find a rag to soak up the mess, but there are more pressing issues calling my attention.

Once again, I'm sitting back on my knees and covering my erection. Elle's eager and pulls me forward until I align with her. The words, asking if she's sure, are sitting on the tip of my tongue, but they never have a chance to be said.

❧

MY ARM IS DEAD. Each time I try to wiggle my fingers, they tingle, and I beg the painful sensation to stop. I look at the beautiful woman holding my arm in place and can't believe we're waking up next to each other. I'm afraid to roll onto my side out of fear I'll wake Elle. As much as I love her, she's a grouch in the morning. No man needs to deal with Elle James without a cup of coffee.

Long gone are my blankets, kicked off the bed in the middle of our night fueled with passion. Her hair covers her back, possibly providing very little warmth. I lift my head to assess the situation I'm in. I'm still naked, and another glance at Elle shows me she's the same. Man, how'd I get so lucky?

After last night, everything has changed for us. The thought brings a smile to my face. Finally, we can be together. No more cat and mouse games. There won't be any more hidden feelings, especially from me. I know how she feels now.

As much as I want my arm back, I don't dare pull it out from under her head. Instead, I inch closer and place my arm over her stomach, nestling into her. For as long as I can remember, Elle's used the same shampoo. She always smells like the sun, beach, and coconut. Even on the rainiest of days, she can walk into a room and change my outlook by the smell of her hair. I close my eyes, content and happy with what's transpired between us.

My hand rests on her stomach, moving up and down with the rise and fall of her breathing. I'm tempted to wake her up, but I also want her to sleep. She needs it. The demons she's been dealing with sometimes get the better of her and right now, Elle seems to be at peace. I put her there, finally showing her how I've felt and how good we can be together. The thought of us staying in bed all day brings a stupid cheesy smile to my face.

Honestly, I can't imagine spending my day any differently.

I pull myself closer, tucking my hand under her breast. She stirs, mumbles something unintelligible and relaxes against me. Right now, in this moment, it's my very own slice of heaven, right here, holding the woman I'm in love with, the morning after. I'm not sure my day, week or month could get any better.

Of course, it can. Elle could come with me to New York. It would mean she'd have to take a quarter off because it's too late to secure an internship, but I'd make it worth her while. I know it's not right for her to stop her education in favor of my dream, but I'll ask her anyway. I'll put the offer out on the table with the promise of late night walks in Central Park, strolls down Fifth Avenue, and shared bags of roasted nuts. We can visit the Statue of Liberty, take the train to Philadelphia or become baseball fans and start going to games. The opportunities to develop our relationship away from the social scene in Los Angeles, are endless. Plus Elle would be closer to Peyton, and with all the wedding planning starting, Elle could be at Peyton's beckon call. All Elle has to do is say yes.

"Just say yes," I whisper against her shoulder. "We can make all our dreams come true together."

Elle stirs, much to my surprise. I honestly expected her to sleep well past noon. She rolls over and into my arms, snuggling into the crook of my neck. I could get used to this. In fact, I think I already am. I mean, who wouldn't? Elle is the woman of my dreams, and here she is, lying in my arms.

"Hmm." Elle's fingers are in my hair, softly weaving in and out.

My leg moves between hers, tangling us together. "Yeah." I sigh, contently and happily.

Elle's body goes rigid. She pushes against my chest until her arms are in the fully locked position. "What're you doing in my bed?"

The smile I've had since I woke up slowly starts to fade. Does she not remember last night? "We're in my bed."

Her head slowly turns, and her eyes dart back and forth wildly. She sits up quickly, her hand instantly going to her head. "Oh, God."

Well, yes you did call out to him a few times last night. I fight the urge to say those words. I sit up and reach for her, but she recoils. Her negative response hits me square in the chest. My mouth goes dry, yet I have a serious need to swallow the pooling saliva in my mouth.

"Shit."

"Elle?" She doesn't look at me. Instead, she scrambles off the bed and tries to dress quickly. I say her name again, but she shakes her head.

"Nothing happened, right? I mean we're naked, but it doesn't mean we slept together. Please tell me we didn't sleep together."

I can't look at her. This can't be happening. My ears must be deceiving me because she's asking me to tell her we didn't have sex when we did. Why is she doing this?

"Ben?" Her voice is full of panic.

I shake my head, almost as if it's an automatic response. "We kissed," I tell her. "But I think we must've passed out. I don't really remember." Except I remember it all. Everything. Every word you said to me. The lie falls easily from my mouth. Her face morphs into something I can only describe as relief. She's happy nothing happened between us and the realization guts me in the stomach. I turn my attention toward the wall, my bed, my bare legs, anywhere but at her. Blindly, I reach behind me and bring my pillow forward to cover myself up. I can't bring myself to look at her, mostly out of fear I might start crying. She doesn't need to see me like this.

"I'm going to go," she says. All I can do is nod because any words I say will make me sound like I have a vise grip squeezing the life out of my family jewels. I'm not sure how long I sit like this. It's long after my front room door closes, long after my back starts aching, and well past the point of a broken heart.

7

ELLE

*T*he soap lathers against my skin, covering me in white suds. I scrub, almost until my skin is raw, needing the pain to numb the thoughts running through my mind. In all the years Ben and I have known each other, and with all the stupid things we have done over those years, I have never woken up naked in his bed. Right now, I can't explain it. Each time I close my eyes, I try to recall what happened last night. I know I was drinking. The wine was going down far too easily, but I'm drawing a blank.

Deep down, I know in my heart Ben would never take advantage of me, but it doesn't explain how I woke up in his arms. Sure, we've slept in the same bed before, but there's always been a pillow between us. I've always stayed on my side, and he his. And we've always kept our clothes on.

"What have I done?" Regretfully, there isn't anyone to give me the answers I need, and I'm not confident in

Ben's answer. He tells me nothing happened, other than we kissed. I touch my lips, wishing I could recall the moment my best friend and I crossed the line. Did I initiate the kiss? If so, I hope it wasn't some sloppy kiss overrun by drool. Ben deserves better, and if I was a drunken idiot, I hope I didn't disappoint him.

However, I've disappointed myself. This is exactly what Quinn said, I need help, and admitting I have a problem is the first step, but do I? I mean, I had some fun at my best friend's birthday party, who's going to fault me for enjoying myself?

"I am," I say aloud. I should've never brought Ben into my messed up world. I know he's been my rock, especially when Peyton had her accident, but I should've shut the door the minute my life started changing.

I rinse off, glance down at my torso, legs, and bring my arms into my line of sight. True to my nature, I've rubbed my skin raw. And for what? To erase the idea of Ben from my skin? That's not right. I shouldn't feel disgusted, but I do. Not because of who he is, but of what I've done.

Without really thinking, I grab my duffel bag and throw some clothes in there. Once I'm dressed, I'm rushing out of my apartment and to my car. Peyton and Noah are here for at least one more day. Not only do I need to spend some time with my sister, but I need to talk to her. She'll know how to fix things with Ben and me.

Thankfully, traffic is minimal and what could've taken me two hours to get to my parents' only takes one. I wish I could say I put my morning behind me, but I can't. Thoughts of Ben's naked body pressing against mine play like a traffic accident on the side of the road. You're not supposed to look, but you do. You stare, craning your head until you can no longer see, and wonder what happened. Who caused the accident? Did anyone die? Did I know anyone?

I'm not likening my morning to an accident at all, however, each time I close my eyes, I can feel Ben behind me, and I can see him in all his glory, and I wish our circumstances were different because I can't look away, no matter how hard I try.

I wipe angrily at the tears streaming down my face. If this isn't a good enough reason to quit drinking, I don't know what is. I can't go through life waking up in beds, not remembering what happened the night before.

As soon as I pull into my parents' driveway, I heave a sigh of relief. No one, besides Peyton, is going to know what happened, and telling her is going to be hard. I don't want to be judged. I'm getting enough of that from Quinn, and supposedly my parents. Of course, walking in today will be a shock to them. I haven't exactly been responsive to their requests.

I don't bother knocking, which I don't exactly recommend. It seems I'm a hot topic of conversation. Instead of making my presence known, I stand back and listen to my family discuss me in detail.

"She's out of control," Dad says.

"She's going through a rough patch," Peyton replies.

"I'm scared of what might happen to her," Mom says.

Noah is the only one not speaking. He's sipping his coffee and looking out over the surf, minding his own business. I'm sure he has an opinion, but he's likely saving it for when he's alone with Peyton.

"Ahem." All four of them turn and look at me. It takes a moment before their shocked expressions morph into smiles. My mom is the first to stand and pull me into her arms. Her hug is genuine, but I'm too pissed to really put much effort into mine.

"We didn't know you were coming down today," she says, appraising me.

"Clearly." I look around, making eye contact with my dad. He stands and pulls me into his arms.

"We only want what's best for you, princess." He kisses the top of my head, and I find myself fighting back the tears. When did I become my own worst enemy?

I bury my face in my dad's neck. Try as I might, it's hard to stay upset with him. I don't know if it's because he's always been there for Peyton and I or if it's simply because he's my dad and right now my heart is breaking at the thought that I've disappointed him.

Growing up, my friends who have step-parents always complained about them, but aside from the normal parental grumbles, I've never said anything bad about mine. As angry as we've been at each other through my teen years, never have I thought about saying the words 'you're not my father' to him. For one, I know it would devastate him and two, saying something to that effect would destroy any relationship we have. My dad has, from the day he entered our lives, always loved Peyton and me as his own.

After my dad pulls away, I look at Peyton. She has tears in her eyes, making me wonder if they're for me or if something is going on with her. I can't imagine her and Noah are fighting. They're ridiculously in love, it's rather sickening.

"P, can I talk to you? Out there." I point toward the beach. It'll give us some privacy, and the sound of the ocean will drown out our voices. She stands and reaches for my hand, linking fingers with mine. Together, we trudge through the sandy beach until we're far enough away from our parents.

We sit, side by side with our legs touching. Peyton reaches for my hand again, almost as if she knows something is wrong. It's our twin thing. When she was in the hospital, I wasn't feeling her pain, but I felt... odd. I knew when she was in the accident something had happened, but I didn't know what.

"What's it like to be perfect?"

Peyton looks at me, but I keep my eyes trained on the surfers riding the waves. "What're you talking about?"

"Everything you do, it's perfect. The way Mom and Dad look at you, the way your relationship with Noah has been. Even Kyle, who was probably in love with you, is your best friend. It doesn't matter what you do or say. You can do no wrong."

"That's not true, Elle. No one sees me as perfect."

"Noah does," I point out.

"Ha. If you think so, you should spend a day in our apartment. He nags me constantly about my socks being on the floor, about how I do the dishes, about how I always leave a glass or plate behind because I don't want to rearrange what I've already put in the dishwasher. I have flaws, E. I have scars like everyone else. No one is perfect and those who strive to be, only let themselves down in the end. And if you think Noah thinks I'm perfect, you should have a long talk with him because I guarantee you, he doesn't."

"But he does. So do Mom and Dad. You walk on water where they're concerned."

Peyton laughs. "I call it guilt. I was living in Chicago while the rest of my family was living here. I was alone, granted, by choice, but when the accident happened, they couldn't reach me for hours. They don't think I'm perfect. They think I'm fragile and on the verge of a nervous breakdown."

"Are you?" I ask, finally looking at her.

She shakes her head. "No, I'm not. I'm in a really good place with Noah. Yes, our schedules suck, and he's giving up a lot to be with me, but I'm trying to make things worth it for him. I know living in Chicago isn't his idea of a good time, but he tries, for me. He's willing to do whatever it takes so I can have the career I want."

"You know you don't have to work once you're married, right?"

Peyton shrugs. "I want to. I want to be on the sidelines calling a game. As odd as it sounds, I want Nick to turn on the television some Sunday and see me there, reporting. I want people to see that despite who my husband is or who my father is, I'm independent and can pave my way."

"And I'm the opposite right now. I feel like no matter what I do, it's wrong. If something is working, I'm looking for a way to break it. I hate school right now. I told Quinn I wanted to drop out and start my career and he fired me before he truly even hired me. He's on my tail about my drinking, grades, and my social life."

"It's what big brothers do."

"But it's not. I need him to be supportive."

"He is, Elle. All of us are, but watching you go through this change is hard. I would understand if we had a sheltered life, but we didn't. We traveled the world on a tour bus. We've been to the Oscars, the Grammy's and a slew of other parties. Dad didn't keep us locked away or hidden from the paparazzi. And I know you went through a lot when I was in that bed, hanging on, but look at me, I'm fine. I'm getting married!"

I do look at her, and all I see is perfection. Somewhere along the lines of growing up, I went from the girl whose daddy called her princess because of how I dressed and acted, to the girl who started acting like her brother and dad, wearing combat boots and flannel shirts tied around my waist. Peyton, who everyone thought would be this tomboy, turned into a girly girl. We became polar opposites of who we were before we hit our teenage years. Part of me wishes I could go back, make a change or two while the other part of me wishes I never had to grow up.

"You are getting married, and I have a feeling it'll be the most perfect wedding ever."

Peyton moves a few strands of hair out of my face. "Elle, to me, you're perfect. You're my sister, my best friend and the only person who knows all my secrets. Even Noah doesn't know everything. I don't know what's going on, but I'm here for you. You can tell me anything, knowing I won't judge. I'll listen and offer what advice I can, but you have to let me in." She pulls me toward her, allowing me to rest my head on her shoulder and for that short moment in time we become us again. Peyton and Elle, twins together taking on the world. Together, we sit and watch the guys surf, oohing and aahing when they do something cool, and chuckling under our breaths when they crash and burn.

8

BEN

*T*he six-pack of beer I carry into my brother's garage isn't going to be enough to dim the memories I have of last night nor will it come close to erasing the horrors I felt this morning. Deep down, I knew I should've put a stop to everything Elle and I were doing last night, but I didn't, and now I'm the one paying the price.

How does she not remember? One would think your body would remember a night of sex. It wasn't some wham bam, catch in the morning romp either. I took care of her, and she, me. We made our first time count, and while she may have been drunk or tipsy when we started, I can guarantee she wasn't by the time we finished. Yet, when the sun rose, she had zero recollection. I don't even want to think how many times she's done this. The thought literally makes me want to hurl.

I set the beer down on the garage floor next to the legs of my brother. He pulls himself out from under the car and smiles. "Two days in a row. I must've done something good in my past life."

"And what were you in your past life?" I ask my brother.

"Hell if I know," he says, sitting upright. He reaches into his pocket and pulls out his keys, where there's a bottle opener. He takes two beers out of the flimsy cardboard carrier, pops the tops, letting the metal clank to the floor and hands me one. "Cheers. So why ya here?"

"Do I need an excuse to visit you?"

Brad pauses briefly before finishing his sip. "I saw you last night at your birthday party getting cozy with Elle." He waggles his eyebrows, which results in me shaking my head. I stand and go over to his current project. About six months ago, some guy asked Brad to rebuild a '65 Mustang for him, offering him a boatload of money and a fancy garage to work in, which he couldn't pass it up.

"What color is she going to be?"

"Cherry red with white leather interior."

"How long until it's finished?" I ask.

Brad comes over to stand next to me. "Once I finish with the engine, I'll start the paint. The seats will be here in a few weeks. I can't sew so I had to outsource them."

"Then what happens then?"

My brother tips his bottle back and finishes his beer, whereas I haven't even touched mine. Honestly, I'm not much of a day drinker, and as much as I'd love to get hammered and forget about the past twenty-four hours, it's just not in me.

"Mr. Berg says he has another project, but he's yet to

say what it is, so we'll see. Never know, maybe you'll have a new roommate soon."

"Or you could sublet," I tell him with a shrug. Brad looks at me expectantly as if he's waiting for me to finish. I sigh and finally take a drink from my bottle of beer. "I've been offered an internship in New York. I have until finals to decide on whether I'm going to take it or not."

"What does Elle say?"

I shake my head. "I haven't told her."

"Why not? You've told her absolutely everything from the day you met her, and you didn't share your big news with her?" This is true. I've told her things she probably shouldn't know, like things about Brad that should've never left our house.

"I don't know. Lately, things between us have felt strained."

Brad shakes his head and returns to the front of the car where he grabs another beer. He holds one up for me, but I show him the one still in my hand, barely touched. "Like I said, last night you and little miss Elle were looking awfully cozy. I saw the way she was touching you and batting her baby blues. Even saw your girl turn green when you were talking to other women."

"I doubt Elle was jealous of anyone speaking to me."

Brad scoffs. "Ben, have you gone on a date since you moved here?" He drops a tool into the toolbox causing a loud clunk, making me jump.

I shrug. "Once or twice. I'm focusing on school."

"Same excuse you used in high school."

"I dated in high school," I retort. Although, not heavily. It was usually a movie date or two, maybe dinner on occasion. Most of the time, I hung out with Elle, Peyton, and our group of friends. We'd party, hang at the beach, have bonfires, some would hook-up, and we'd repeat everything the next weekend.

"Right, what was her name? Elise?"

"Ella," I mutter. For months, everyone gave me crap for dating Ella because her name was so close to Elle's. Sadly, our relationship didn't last too long because I referred to Ella as Elle one too many times. Their names were just so close it was an easy mistake. I vowed never to make the same one again when it came to dating someone with the same name.

"Oh right. I remember Mom even called her Elle at dinner. That was awkward. Elle used to think it was all fun and games."

Elle thinks life is a game most of the time. Brad and I make eye contact, but that's it. I don't shrug or try to think of a comeback.

"What's wrong?" he asks.

"Elle and I slept together last night."

"Right on, bro!" Brad sticks his hand up for high five, but I shake my head. His arm slowly drops, as does the expression on his face.

"Maybe she was drunk, maybe not. She told me she wasn't."

"Is she saying you raped her?"

I quickly shake my head. "No, nothing like that. She doesn't remember."

"You're joking?"

I bring my bottle of beer up to my lips again, and this time I guzzle the contents down. Brad quickly hands me another with the top already popped. I drink about half before I feel like I have the confidence to face my brother with the most fucked up story of my life. "I wish I were. Last night was..." I pause, realizing Brad doesn't need to hear the fluffy details about my encounter. "This morning, she freaked out when she woke up naked and asked me what happened. There was something about the way she looked at me and her voice. This feeling in my gut told me she was afraid we had crossed the line, so I lied and told her we kissed, but didn't do the deed."

"But you did?"

"Many times."

"And she doesn't remember?"

I take a long pull and finish this bottle as well. Brad goes to get me my third, but I wave him off. "Has this ever happened to you?"

Brad laughs but quickly stops. "Sorry, man. Nah, can't say it has. I get the job done."

"I got the job done, Brad. I have the scratch marks to prove it." I turn and lift my shirt up. My brother utters some profanities before whipping me with a towel. I cry out and dodge his next maneuver. "Be serious for five seconds. I don't know how you get so many chicks."

Brad holds his arms out to the side. "It's the bad boy image. Put some gel in your hair, act like you don't give a shit and they come flocking to you with their daddy issues."

"Somehow I don't think gel is going to make Elle come running."

"So forget her," Brad says. He leans up against the car, his coveralls stained with paint and grease. "Honestly, it's time to move on, Ben. This is your wake-up call. You slept with the chick you've been in love with for years, and she dogged you first thing. If that doesn't scream friend zone, I don't know what does. It's time to pull up your big boy pants and get the hell out of dodge. Where'd you say your internship is?"

"New York."

"Take it and run. Get out of California and explore the world for both of us. You don't want to end up like me, working in some old man's garage, praying he'll have another car for me to fix so I can eat."

"You know you could always come live with me."

Brad shakes his head. "Nah, you need peace and quiet so you can graduate and become something. I'm good here, watching you succeed." Brad heads to his toolbox and rifles through it until he finds whatever he needs. We've never really discussed our differences. While we look alike, we have different fathers, and while mine left me with a trust fund, which I can't touch until after graduation, his father has always been absent. I think this is why Brad followed me to California when I moved out here for college, so I always had him.

"If I go, my apartment will be free for six weeks."

"I got a bed here. You should sublet it and make some money back, and then take that money and find a nice girl to spend it on who doesn't go by Elle James. She doesn't deserve you, Ben. She never has."

"You say that, but you like her." I point out.

Brad nods. "I do. Elle's a cool chick. So is Peyton. But liking her and thinking she's the best fit for my baby brother are two different things." Brad drops down onto his creeper and pulls himself under the car. A sure signal our conversation is over. I try to linger and even look around for something to do, but this is where Brad and I differ greatly. He's good with his hands, while I'm creative with my mind.

"I'll see," I say loud enough for him to hear.

"Call me when you need a ride to the airport. I'll take you."

"Thanks."

As soon as I pull away from the garage, I drive toward the beach. It's early spring, a Saturday and the traffic is going to be a pain, but it'll give me time to think and process everything Brad said. As much as I don't want to admit it, he's right. I need to move on. I need to do what's right for me. I think last night had to happen to bring me to this point. Elle and I are on two different pages. She wants to party and hook-up. I want to graduate and start a career and a life with someone I'm in love with. That's something we can't do together.

It takes me almost two hours, but my toes are finally in the sand. Of course, everywhere I look there are couples, chasing each other, making out or walking hand in hand along the shore, making me feel like I'm missing out on something very important in life.

The thing is, as hard as I try, I can't imagine myself with anyone other than Elle. I've tried, and maybe it's because she's always there, living next door, barging into my apartment, calling me at all hours of the night. I can't escape her, even if I tried.

And I really need to try.

I pull my phone out of my pocket and turn it on. It

comes to life with messages from classmates thanking me for the party, but nothing from Elle. Honestly, I didn't expect her to text or even call. What would she even say? I knew better than to sleep with her, yet I went ahead and did it anyway because I'm stupidly in love with her and now I'm going to be the one to pay the price. That price will be our friendship because I don't know if I can go on pretending like nothing happened between us, and I definitely don't know if I can turn a blind eye when she brings another guy home.

9

ELLE

"YAHOO!"

SLOWLY, I open my eyes and let the sunlight in. There's another joyous scream coming from somewhere outside, and for some odd reason, I'm smiling. I don't know why. Maybe it's because I'm home with my family, and when I'm here, everything feels right in my life.

Sometime before dinner last night, Quinn showed up, making my parents beyond happy to have us all home. Our dad insisted on firing up the grill and building a bonfire, something we really haven't done in awhile. With Peyton living in Chicago, it's been hard for her to come here as often as we want, especially now that Noah lives with her as well. As a family, we needed these past hours to reconnect and just be the Powell-James clan we're used to being.

I thought for sure once Peyton and I came back to the house after sitting on the beach, my parents would say something about my party habits. They didn't. My dad pulled me into his arms though, and I broke down. Even though he didn't utter a single word, I could feel the love pouring through him. I guess right now I need strong doses of hard love, and he's going to give it to me. Mom, on the other hand, fussed over everything, asking if I was eating right, studying hard and sleeping at least eight hours. I think that was her subtle way of telling me she's watching. Through Quinn, no less. Those two have been thick as thieves from day one.

The living room is empty, and the glass wall that leads to the beach is wide open, letting in a nice breeze, along with more laughter. I step out onto the patio and use my hand to block the sun to seek out the source of the noise. Not far from the house is my family, creating an early morning ruckus. I think about staying back and watching, or even slipping out to return home, but I want to be with them, at least for one more day. Tomorrow, reality can rear its ugly head and destroy what's remaining of my life.

As soon as I touch the sand with my bare feet, I sigh. Normally, the sand is too hot to walk in without shoes, so this is nice. I stop and look down at my feet and wiggle my toes, giggling loudly. I find myself walking briskly toward my family. They're sitting together, spread out on multiple blankets, not far from shore. This is my parents' happy place, and honestly, I find solace here too. The beach is calm and perfect unless it's storming. However, a good storm on the beach is a remarkable sight.

Noah's the first one to see me. He's standing there with only shorts on and a football in his hand and waves in my direction. "Morning."

"Morning," I say as I approach. I sit down next to my mom who puts her arm around me.

"There are breakfast burritos in the bag there." Mom points to a line of bags filled with various foods and a few coolers.

Confusion clouds my face as I look at her. "We live at the beach." I point to our house. "Are you not able to walk back and forth?"

Mom shrugs. Dad laughs. "No, she's not. Your mother hates it, so she makes me bring as much out as possible." Dad hands me a still wrapped burrito. "The food truck was down the way earlier this morning, so Quinn and I grabbed everyone something to eat and, by the way, good morning, princess," he says, kissing me on the cheek. His wetsuit is hanging around his waist. One of the arms swings wildly, hitting me in the face.

"Morning, Daddy." I don't care how old I am he will always be "daddy" to me. There's something about the way his eyes light up when either Peyton or I call him that, that I never want to see fade.

"Your wetsuit's by your board," he says.

When I came down yesterday, I had every intention of going back and didn't bring a change of clothes with me. However, the thought of seeing Ben last night didn't sit very well with me, and I kept procrastinating and finding reasons to stay. When Quinn showed up, it was just nice to be with my family, and I ended up staying, and while I do have a few things here, the essentials are at home.

"Maybe later." I hold up the burrito even though I'm not sure I want to eat it.

"Come on, E." Peyton stands and tugs on my hand.

"I don't have a swimsuit with me." It's an excuse. I could always go in my bra and panties, but what an uncomfortable ride home that would be. It's something Peyton, and I have done many times, and it's not my favorite option.

"I bought you some new things the other day when I was shopping," my mom says. I glance at her, but she doesn't seem fazed. This is probably something she could've mentioned yesterday.

"What's the occasion?"

"She was shopping with Peyton," Quinn interjects. "And she feels guilty if she buys something for just one of us."

I nod. "Score one for the guilt tripped parent." Quinn and I bump fists and laugh.

"I feel like I'm losing out on getting new things," Noah says, causing us all to laugh.

"I bought you the football," Mom says, adding a smirk.

"I think that's what we used to call a burn, babe," Peyton says to Noah, who is standing there with his mouth wide open. He finally closes it and shakes his head.

"Thanks, Mom." I lean into her and let her hold me. I

have a feeling today is going to be one of those days I don't want to end, and tomorrow's going to be the day I never want to arrive because I have to go back to being Elle James, the party girl, and we all know the party girl doesn't change overnight. Except this one wants to because she has an unsettling feeling she's really screwed up with her best friend and doesn't know how to fix things.

"Where's the food?" I look up in time to see our uncle Jimmy walk across our blankets and head right toward the bags.

"Back at your house," Dad says, pushing his friend and bandmate away from our stash.

"I tried to feed him at home, but he said your food is going to be better," Jenna places a few bags down and shakes her head. She says hi to all of us before taking a seat next to my mom.

"Where's Eden?" I ask. Jenna points toward the surf, where Eden is standing with her surfboard under her arm. "Who's the guy?"

"Some bloke who's not worth the time of day," Jimmy says through gritted teeth.

My eyes go from Jimmy to Jenna, who is shaking her head, and then back to Eden, whose head is thrown back in what I'm gathering is flirtatious laughter. I glance at Noah, who has finally sat down next to my sister. "Are your parents coming?"

He shakes his head. "Nah. I didn't really think this was turning into a family reunion."

"When isn't it?" I ask.

"She has a point," Quinn says,

Jimmy sits down next to Jenna. I lean forward and say, "So the kid... not a fan, Jimmy?"

He pauses mid-bite and shakes his head. If I'm not mistaken, I believe he's let out a growl. I try not to laugh, but can't hold back.

"This is payback for all the womanizing he did before we got married," Jenna says.

"You're not helping, sweet lips."

"Just saying, Jimmy. What comes around goes around." Jenna shrugs and turns toward my mom, hiding the massive smile on her face.

"Jenna's right, JD. Think about all those tours—"

"Flying burrito," Quinn yells just as Jimmy's half-eaten breakfast lands on our dad's bare chest.

Every single one of us starts to laugh. Peyton snorts, which makes us all roar. And over all of our noise, Jimmy is yelling at our dad in some unintelligible British language, though I definitely picked up a few curse words.

"What's so funny?"

We all stop and straighten up as Eden stares at us.

"Come eat, honey," Jenna says, reaching for her daughter. Eden slams her board into the sand and ignores her mother's hand. Jenna frowns but looks down at the ground so no one sees it. Ah, the teenage years of thinking you don't need either of your parents only to lie awake at night, wishing you could tell them all your secrets because the burden is too much. I remember those days well.

As soon as everyone's done with breakfast, I run back to the house and change into one of my older swimsuits. I don't care how many times it's been through the wash, it still smells like sun and sand. Back outside, I look at my family, wishing Ben was with us, but I've ruined things there. I have a feeling my family knows something is up because no one has asked where he is this weekend. Normally, he'd be with me and be part of my family.

Down in the water, everyone but my mom and Jenna are hitting the waves. I stand back and watch Eden, who is better than any of us. "Wow, she's amazing."

"She wants to go professional," Jenna says. "Jimmy and I aren't sure because of the time she'd have to devote."

"You'd have to travel a lot, I'm sure," my mom adds.

Jenna nods. "Hawaii and Australia, mostly. There's plenty of competitions here, but she would have to train year around. I don't know. I think she should wait. Jimmy doesn't say much because either I'm the one who moves with her or he has to quit the band. Eden hates us right now because we can't make a decision."

My mom pulls Jenna into her arms, consoling her. I have a hard enough time with the life-changing decision I'm trying to make. I can't imagine being faced with one that changes your entire family.

I give the rest of my family my attention, watching as they ride the waves. My dad, Quinn, and Eden ride flawlessly, while Noah and Jimmy fall off, and Peyton never stands on her board, choosing to paddle back in.

"You coming out, princess?" my dad asks as soon as he's back on the shore.

"I don't know. Watching Eden, I feel like I'm not very good."

Eden laughs but doesn't say anything. She drops her board in the water and paddles back out.

I'm on the cusp of making my decision when I'm picked up from behind. I scream, my arms flail and I try to hang out, but to no avail. I'm dropped into the ocean with barely enough time to hold my breath. I come up, sputtering with my hair covering my face. When I finally move the rat's nest from my eyes, my brother is standing in front of me with his board.

"Bet you can't catch me," he says before tossing his board onto the water and paddling away.

"Ugh!" I groan, much to the delight of my family, who are laughing again.

After hours of surfing, playing volleyball, laying in the sun, eating and napping every chance we can, Quinn and Noah have started up the bonfire again, and the parental units cook dinner. Peyton and I are sitting side by side, watching the guys.

"I thought you had to fly home today?"

"We did," Peyton says. "But Noah thought we could use another day. We'll leave in the morning. Private jet and all."

"The perks." I sigh as if it's so bad to have a private jet at our disposal. Peyton and I start laughing, likely thinking the same thing, which causes Noah and Quinn to look over at us. "He loves you, you know."

"How can you tell?" she asks.

"It's the way he looks at you, the way he watches you. He's always smiling. And he knows where you are at all times. While everyone was on the beach today, you walked up behind him. I thought for sure he was going to scream, but it's like he knew you were there the whole time. He didn't even flinch."

"He's my dream come true, Elle."

"Your fairy tale?"

"My happily ever after. He's my best friend. He's part of my soul, and without him, I don't feel complete. Noah's my forever."

I reach for my sister's hand, holding it tightly. It wasn't too long ago that I begged the man who she's about to marry to let her go, to tell my sister goodbye. Every day I thank God he never listened to me.

10

BEN

From my parking spot, I stare at my second-floor bedroom window with an uneasy feeling, or maybe it's dread. I'm not really sure at this point because I've never felt like I've had the weight of the world on my shoulders for something as trivial as sex, especially with my best friend. Any guy worth his nuts would've come clean when asked and probably boasted about the fact the deed was done, but that's not me, and now I'm wondering how to make it through the next few weeks until I can leave because I'm definitely leaving once I tell my professor my decision.

I just can't seem to bring myself to make the phone call or walk to his office after class today. My one good bit of luck for today is that he wasn't teaching and his aid was, which meant I didn't have to face Jacobs.

The truth is, I'd be an idiot for giving up this opportunity. I don't care if the internship is for one quarter, that's weeks of knowledge that could catapult my career. I'd have my foot in the door at one of the most prestigious marketing firms in the country with a job offer likely when I graduate. So why am I so hesitant to accept? My decision on whether to go or not shouldn't be based on what my best friend or former BFF is going to do when I'm gone or what she's going to think. Honestly, Elle should be happy, beyond ecstatic, that I'm even a candidate for this position.

The thing about living in the same complex is I can never escape Elle, until this weekend, that is. I thought for sure I'd run into her each time I went outside, but I didn't. Never mind she never contacted me. I don't know if I was expecting her to call me in the middle of the night like she normally does or what. Stupidly, I stayed up, waiting and thinking about what I would say to her. All night I replayed the conversation we'd have. I'd tell her everything and ask her for a chance, showing my brother he's wrong about Elle. Of course, I had the opposite conversation too, with her telling me we'd never be anything more than friends. Unfortunately, this is the last thought I had before I went to sleep, which is just another reason why I need to let Elle go.

After my last class, I head home. Normally, I'd spend some time in the library because getting homework done at home is near impossible. As my luck would have it, there's a party at the pool, evident by the number of giggles and splashing I can hear.

This apartment complex is full of students, so it's not uncommon for people to gather at the pool this close to spring break, but still a distraction I don't need with finals coming up.

It isn't until I round the corner do I see Elle. I stand back in the shadows, watching her. She's dressed in a hot pink bikini, one I haven't seen before, but I like it. The color compliments her tan skin. She has a group of girls with her, who are all dancing in the water to the music playing. Each one has a drink in their hand. I'm curious about what Elle's drinking from her in Nalgene bottle, but I don't dare ask. I need to separate myself from her life, and this is one way to start.

Squaring my shoulders, I keep my head down and pretend like I'm completely oblivious to the world around me. If this were last week, I'd go right over to the pool and take part in the festivities for a little while before going up to my apartment. The new me can't do that.

"Ben!" I'd know her voice from anywhere. It pains me to face her, knowing she doesn't remember what happened between us.

I stop and wave in a half-assed attempt at being civil when all I really want to do is run upstairs and hide behind my closed door. Everything Brad said to me about letting her go rushes to my mind as I smile or grimace, depending on who's looking. What my brother didn't say is that I'm a weak-minded man when it comes to Elle James. She controls just about every single aspect of me, and she knows it.

"Come join us," Elle beckons.

I have one foot on the step, and the other pointed toward her, both wanting to go in their own direction and neither making the decision any easier.

"Yeah, come on, Ben." One of Elle's friends waves me over. I'd love to be any other guy right now because a swimming pool full of women is literally every guy's dream. Except for mine, because I only want one person and she doesn't want me back.

"Sorry, I need to study. Big final coming up." The girls laugh. I'm not sure who, but there's definitely more than one giggling at my statement, which makes my decision an easy one. My brain wins out while my heart berates me for my decision. I take the stairs two at a time, cognizant of Elle calling my name.

With my front door closed, I lean against it, wishing the music downstairs would shut off, and the women would leave. But it won't happen. Quinn will come home, and Elle will bat her blue eyes until he starts up the grill. The pool party will expand, and everyone will get in on the social soirée. Everyone but me because doing so would only put me back to square one, and I need to move on.

Homework is the only thing that will get my mind off the party outside. My books are spread out in front of me and my laptop's open. The blank white page and black cursor are waiting for my infinite wisdom and the social economic change in business when a new president is elected. I'm supposed to take an unbiased approach, which I'm not sure anyone can.

As soon as I put my headphones on and turn on my music, I start typing and quickly lose track of time. It's dusk when I stand and stretch, making my way to the kitchen. The refrigerator is empty and all the food left over from my birthday party was spoiled when I didn't put it away. "What a waste," I say to myself, although I don't know if I'm talking about the food, the party or the night with Elle. I suppose it's all three combined.

I take out my last remaining beer and pop the top before heading toward the window, which is framed by the curtains that came with the apartment. They used to be white but have turned some sickly cream or yellowish color after years of hanging from the same rod.

I pull one to the side as stealthily as possible, except there isn't anything remotely coy about what I'm doing. Anyone watching will see my curtain move, and if they study hard enough, they'll see me standing there, lurking like a freaking peeping tom.

From what I can see, the party has doubled in size, and now the women are playing volleyball. Elle's sitting on the edge of the pool with her long legs in the water. She points and laughs and my stomach aches. What I wouldn't give to be carefree like her, to not have a care in the world. That'll never be me, not in this lifetime.

I could go down there and act like Elle, pretend like nothing is wrong, like nothing has happened between us. Technically, that's what I told her, so why should she believe otherwise.

I should've been honest with her from the beginning, back when I started developing feelings for her, but I held myself in check and enjoyed our friendship. Now look at me, I'm hiding in my apartment because I can't face her.

My life has become a barrage of things I should've, could've or would've done. I guess that's why hindsight is fifty-fifty. Once you've made a choice or mistake, you're like damn, here's a laundry list of ways things could've been different.

My shoulder aches from the way I'm leaning against the wall, but I ignore the pain and continue to spy on the party. Every few minutes someone else shows up, but it isn't until Quinn steps into the pool area do the gaggle of women start calling out his name. Jealousy fills me, even when it shouldn't. Quinn's one of my best friends and does nothing to warrant envy from me, but I can't help it. I'm not smooth or a chick magnet like he is, and sometimes I wish I were.

My phone rings, causing me to let go of the curtain. The caller ID says "Rolf Jacobs." Do I answer or do I go back to fantasizing about being downstairs. My conscience gets the better of me. "Hello?"

"Mr. Miller, this is Professor Jacobs. Am I catching you at a bad time?"

"No, sir, just reviewing my notes for the upcoming final." I might as well earn some brownie points while I can.

"I've always admired your work ethic, Ben, which is why I put your name in the hat for the internship. Which also brings me to why I'm calling."

For some dumb reason, I open my curtains and stand in my window. If Elle were to look up here, she'd see me, but some guy has her attention. His hand touches her leg, and she doesn't move it, nor does she shy away from him. In this moment, I make my decision.

"Yes, you need to know if I'm going to take the position, right?"

"I do. I don't think I have to say it would be foolish to pass this up. It's truly a once in a lifetime opportunity to work with the best in the business. Not to mention, the pool of students is stellar. You're in good company, Ben."

"Thank you, Professor, for nominating me. I'd be honored to fill the spot."

"Well, that's wonderful news. When I didn't hear right away, I feared you were going to pass."

Believe me, I thought about it.

"No, sir. I only needed some time to process everything and try to figure out what to do with my apartment while I'm living in New York."

"If I can help in any way, let me know. I'll facilitate the necessary paperwork and get you in contact with your manager in New York. Ben, I don't have to tell you what a successful internship will do for your career—"

"No, sir, you definitely don't." I move away from the window, unable to watch the flirting going on downstairs. After my professor and I hang up, I'm left to listen to the party or get the hell out of here. Option B it is.

As quickly as possible, I head down the stairs, unable to avoid the action. My name's called again, but I disregard it, choosing to ignore her instead. It kills me to do this, but she's left me with no choice. If I'm going to pursue my dreams, I need to put Elle on the back burner for now because not doing so will only make me long for a relationship I can't have, at least not with her.

11

ELLE

"*L*ast year, your professors gave you a pass due to the situation with your sister, but according to this report, your grades are barely above passing."

My advisor tosses a sheet of paper onto his desk and leans back in his chair. He steeples his fingers, and I can't tell from where I'm sitting if they're touching his mouth or not. He looks like a police officer, giving an interrogation, yet I've done nothing wrong unless you count being a terrible student, focused on everything other than school. George Tesh has been my advisor from day one, kissing my dad's ass the minute we stepped onto campus at the beginning of my senior year. It was the worst display of brown-nosing I have ever witnessed, and believe me, I've seen a lot.

"This is normally where you give a response," he says.

I shrug. "I don't know what you expect me to say.

Guilty as charged. I haven't taken my studies seriously this year."

"And why is that?"

Who does this man think he is, my dad? It's not a crime to slack off in school. It's not like I'm on scholarship or grants. My parents pay for my tuition, so if anyone should have a problem with my grades, it should be them, yet I don't see them sitting here.

"I'm not sure I have a valid answer for you."

"You do realize graduation is coming and at this rate, you won't walk with your class."

I say nothing.

George leans forward, his chair propelling him forward causing him to slam his hands down on top of his desk. Papers scatter as he tries to right himself. I stifle a laugh, but the scowl on his face tells me he's not impressed.

"Listen, Elle. We were all sympathetic to the situation with your sister, but from what I understand, she's doing well and is thriving in her own studies."

How does he know this? What's he doing, stalking my sister on the WAG's of the NFL?

"We'd like to see the same for you."

"I'm sure my parents would as well."

George sighs. "Which brings me to another point. I spoke with your father—"

"Dad," I say, interrupting him.

"I'm sorry?"

Why do people say "I'm sorry" when they don't understand something? Shouldn't they say, "Can you please repeat yourself" or "What do you mean?" Telling me, he's sorry does nothing for him or me.

"For what?" I counter.

This time the sigh George lets out is so overly exaggerated his lips bounce off each other. I wonder if he has kids, and if so, whether they're girls? My uncles say girls are the worst to raise.

"I don't understand why you corrected me in reference to your father."

"Oh, because he's my dad, not my father. It's a long story and one I'm not willing to share right now, but would appreciate it if you referred to my dad... well, as my dad."

George shakes his head. I get it, it's complicated, but it's mine and Peyton's complication, and we're pretty adamant that the parental distinction stays in place.

"As I was saying, I spoke with your dad..." he looks, maybe for confirmation? I nod and smile, waiting for him to continue. George clears his throat. "As you can probably assume, he's worried about you and your grades and asked that we do whatever we can to get you back on track and prepared for your quarter-final."

"That won't be necessary."

"Unfortunately, you don't have a choice in the manner, Elle. As of right now, you're on academic probation."

"Meaning what exactly?"

"Meaning, moving forward you must attend and pass each and every class. You are also required to attend mandatory study and tutoring session."

"You're kidding, right?"

He shakes his head. "No, I'm not. Elle, you're a good student who has had a rush of bad luck. You still have time to fix your grades and graduate with your class, but you have to put in the work. Your dad agrees."

"This is unbelievable." I'm on the verge of tears and do everything I can to keep them at bay. George Tesh doesn't need to see my weaknesses.

"It's for the best. If you choose not to participate in the plan, you'll be expelled at the beginning of next quarter."

I have to bite the inside of my cheek to keep from lashing out. Something tells me this guy is trying to win my dad over. This feels like George is going above and beyond for his own cause. Who cares if I want to drop out of school or fail? Shouldn't that be my choice or one I make with my parents?

"Am I done here?"

"Sure," he says, nodding.

As soon as I'm out of the building, my phone is to my ear. It rings three times before my dad's voice answers. "How could you do this to me?"

"Hello, Dad. Even though I saw you the other day, I miss you terribly."

I roll my eyes. "Be serious."

"I'm always serious when it comes to you, and your sister and brother. You're my life. You know this."

"But why this? Your brown-nosing buddy is threatening to expel me."

"I know, and believe me, your mom and I thought long and hard about it, but things have to change, Elle. You can't continue down this path. It's not healthy."

"I'm not doing anything wrong," I say through my clenched jaw. "Why couldn't we talk about this when I was home?"

My dad sighs and I can tell he's moving from wherever he is to another room. He's probably in the studio, which means he dropped whatever the band is doing or working on to take my call. That thought has my tears flowing. Most of my friends don't have parents like I do, I should be grateful and appreciative of what they're doing for me.

"Princess, it's not that your mom and I think you're doing anything wrong. We're concerned with the partying and your grades. Before Peyton's accident, you were a straight-A student, on the Dean's List, and receiving awards. Now—"

"Now I'm just a giant fu—"

"Don't you dare finish that sentence, Elle James."

"But it's true, right, Daddy?" A sob breaks out before I have a chance to cover my mouth in order to hold it in. I can disappoint everyone around me, but it kills me to think my parents might feel this way about me.

"Elle, you're lost at the moment, nothing more."

"Well, maybe I can't be found."

"Now you know I don't believe that for a second."

"But what if I am, Daddy?"

"I won't let you be. I'll do what I have to, to find you and bring you back from whatever it is that's going on. I can't even imagine what you experienced when Peyton was lying in that hospital bed. To see your twin sister like that, it had to be the hardest thing you've ever gone through. We each coped a different way, and thinking back, your mom and I should've put you and Quinn into some sort of therapy."

"Quinn? Why him, he's perfect."

"He's not, and he suffered as well. We all did, and once we knew Peyton was going to be okay, we sort of went back to our lives, or at least we've tried to. I often lie awake at night, wondering what she's doing, what you and Quinn are doing. As a parent, you never stop worrying. You never forget the bad things."

"I haven't forgotten."

"I know. For as long as I live, I'll never fully understand the bond you share with Peyton."

"It's a twin thing," I tell him. "We can't explain it."

"And no one is asking you to, but what your mom and I are demanding is an effort. Your grades are not acceptable, Elle. The partying has to stop. I understand wanting to hang out with your friends on the weekends, I get it, but school comes first."

"Or what?" I hedge.

My dad sighs. "You'll be cut off. We will no longer fund your education or your apartment. If Quinn chooses to allow you to live there, it'll be his choice."

"All because I'm getting bad grades? That doesn't seem fair."

"It's not, but we don't know how else to get through to you."

I look around campus, watching as my peers enjoy the springtime sun, wishing I could be out there. I could if I want to defy my dad. My tears start to flow heavily, and my heart aches. It's not broken but damaged. The one person I want to lean on is not returning my calls, and I know, deep down, it has to do with last weekend. I woke up naked and in his bed, yet he tells me nothing happened. I'm not buying his story, but don't have the guts to ask him to tell me the truth, mostly out of fear of what the truth is. If Ben and I have crossed the line, I don't know how I'll forgive myself for putting him in that situation.

"Daddy..." I can't finish my sentence without another sob taking over.

"I know, princess. Believe me, it breaks my heart to say these things to you, but I don't know what else to do. I'm worried about you and think you need some help. If you want to take the last two quarters off and go on a retreat, we can set that up."

"I'm not a drug addict." My words sound hollow.

"No one is saying you are."

"But you want to send me away."

"No, Elle, we want to get you the help you need in order to succeed. Right now, you're your own worst enemy, and you're self-destructing. I'm sorry, but I won't stand by and watch you ruin your life. You won't be a Hollywood statistic."

"Is that what you're worried about, your image?"

My dad groans and I picture him rubbing his hand over his face. It's what he does when he's frustrated. "No, but I'm worried about yours. You aspire to be something in this crazy industry, and as much as I've pushed for you and Quinn to seek out different careers, you're both hell-bent on working in music. I've supported this, against my better judgment, but if you think your name is going to get you places, you're mistaken. Currently, social media presence is everything and right now, your image is that of a party girl. Is that what you want prospective clients to see?"

He said prospective clients, which makes me believe he has faith in my ability to lead a music group to stardom. It's what I want most, especially after the way my dad's band was treated early on. I have notes on their former manager, Sam, on how not to act and conduct business, and have vowed to be better than she was personally and professionally. One thing's for sure; I'll never get involved with my talent. Crossing that line would be worse than crossing it with my best friend.

"No, it's not."

"Then fix it, Elle. Get serious about life and your future."

"What if it's too late?"

"It's not. Just do what Mr. Tesh says; go to the tutoring sessions, meet with the groups and participate. Your grades are what they are this quarter, but next quarter they can be better. Right now, all your mom and I want is for you to be happy, healthy and to pass this current quarter. If you fail a class, it has to be made up before graduation."

"I know," I say meekly.

"Elle, your mom and I love you more than words. We only want the best for you, and if that best isn't college, tell us now so we can help you transition into a different field."

"Okay." The right answer would be for me to tell him I want to stay in school, but the truth of the matter is, I don't know that I do. Right now, I hate it, and maybe it's because I need a break or something, but this place fills me with so much dread, it's like I'm on autopilot. I show up because I'm supposed to, but mentally I'm completely checked out.

"I suppose I ought to get to class."

"That's probably best."

"I love you, Dad." I hang up before he can respond. I've cried enough in the last half hour or so, hearing him tell me he loves me will surely rip my heart to shreds. Before I even move, I send a text to Ben, asking him if he wants to have dinner tonight. I wait for the chat bubbles to appear, but they don't. I have a feeling this message will go unanswered like my phone calls.

BEN

Oddly, I feel at peace with the decision I've made about the internship. Happy, even. I'm looking forward to the challenges that lie ahead, but also terrified I won't live up to the standards my professor is holding me to.

Right now, I'm trying to pass my final. I wish I could say my mind is clear and completely focused on the task at hand, but it's not. It's having an internal battle with my aching and likely broken heart. I want to tell Elle about the offer, but the nagging fear that she'll negate my success plays a huge part in why I haven't said anything. What kind of friend does that make me? A shitty one, if you ask me. For all of Elle's faults, her qualities are double. She's just lost right now.

Which is why I haven't told her. She's dealing with enough of her stuff to have to worry about what I'm doing, and it's not like I'm a priority for her. The text messages she's sent me the past few days have all been complaints about her teachers, classes and her parents. Not a single one asking how I'm doing or where I've been. Even her phone calls are straight to the point, "Call me."

I can't.

Elle James is a weakness I need to overcome.

Yet, I wish she were with me right now, helping me pick out a new wardrobe. Brad used to tease me about my savings, telling me I can't take the money with me so I might as well spend it. My rainy-day fund is coming in handy. According to the packet of papers Professor Jacobs gave me, the dress code is business professional. The bonus is, Fridays are the firm's casual day, which means I can dress down slightly in something like a button-down or sweater vest.

I laugh aloud in the store, garnering odd looks from a few of the other patrons. I can't help but think about Elle's reaction to a sweater vest. One Christmas her father wore one, and I thought the world was ending. Granted, it was an ugly Christmas one, but still, Elle was beside herself, calling Harrison an old fogey. She had everyone in stitches, laughing at the way she was dissing Harrison, even Katelyn.

"May I help you?" the store clerk asks as he straightens out the vest I so haphazardly placed back on the pile.

"I need to buy some work clothes."

"Of course, and where will you be working?"

Working. I'm going to have a job, in the real world. As that thought settles over me, I'm forced to take a deep calming breath. When did I grow up and become an adult? Wasn't it just yesterday, when I shyly approached the twins at school? That day was life-changing. When the twins could've shunned the new kid, they didn't.

"Hey, do you remember the assignment we have for Mrs. Rudolph's class?" I ask the beautiful girl that sits in front of me in biology. I came up with this icebreaker last night while lying in bed. I figure if I can ask her about our homework, she'll talk to me. It may be the third day of my freshman year, but I'm already smitten.

She looks at me without breaking her stride. "I don't have a class with Mrs. Rudolph."

"Third period. Biology." I leave out the part where we'll have to partner up when we study the human anatomy. She approaches her locker, which isn't where I thought it was yesterday. Maybe she requested to have it moved? Is someone bullying her? I could step in if that's the case. My brother Brad and I don't stand for that type of crap. Once she pops the lock and opens the door, I see it's completely covered in pictures of some football player. "Boyfriend?" Please say no. Please say no.

She pauses and looks at the door. "Friend," she mumbles.

Thank you!

"So about our homework?"

She slams the door. "I think you have me confused with my sister." She turns to walk down the hall, making me rush after her. I'm about a foot taller than her, forcing me to look down at the top of her head. Being the smooth teen I am, I step in front of her and backpedal down the hall. My ego's hurt a bit by the annoyed look on her face.

"Can I help you with something?" she asks, stopping in the middle of the hallway.

"Hey, Peyton, do you know if your dad is touring soon?" another girl asks. The gorgeous girl in front of me rolls her eyes and mutters no. The classmate doesn't say anything before walking away. So, her name's Peyton. Different, but I like it.

I make the mistake of watching her classmate and almost lose Peyton slipping by me. However, I'm undeterred and quickly catch up. I follow her to the loud cafeteria because I've been so determined to speak with her, I haven't stopped at my locker to dump my books and grab my lunch. It's okay. I can eat later.

"Hey, this guy is looking for you." Peyton steps out of the way, and that's when my eyes land on another version of Peyton. I don't want to say she's prettier, but... yeah, she is, and the way she's looking at me with her Caribbean blue eyes has my heart beating faster than it ever has and my throat feels like it's closing. Great, I lay eyes on the woman of my dreams, and I'm going to die.

"I'm Benjamin Miller." I stick my hand out for her to shake it. She does, placing her dainty hand in mine. The moment my large hand engulfs her, I don't want to let go, but she pulls away quickly, leaving me wanting more.

"I'm Elle Powell-James, and this is my sister, Peyton."

Elle. Her name is Elle.

My mouth opens and closes, only to open again and say the dumbest thing ever. "Twins," I say stupidly. I mean, of course, they are. They're freaking identical in every way except how they dress. No wonder I messed up. I glance at the both of them, trying to find a distinguishing *feature so I don't make the same mistake again. I have nothing, except for the way Elle smiles. Her head tilts to the side and her eyes, they shine brighter than the northern star. Okay, stop Ben, before you embarrass yourself.*

"So how long have you been in Beaumont?" Elle asks.

"A couple of weeks. We just moved here from Orlando."

"Disneyworld!" the twins say in unison.

"Sorry," Peyton tells me. "We love Disneyworld. It's our favorite place. Our dad takes us there all the time." *They seem sort of old to enjoy a theme park, but who am I to judge. Given a chance, I'd probably go because let's be real, we all want to act like kids.*

"Beaumont must seem like a sleepy little town compared to Orlando. Why'd you move?" Peyton asks.

"We're adjusting." *The truth is, it's a nice change of pace. Orlando was a hectic lifestyle, and we rarely saw our mother. At least here, she's home every night, and we can be a family.*

"What do you like to do?" Elle asks.

I shrug. "Everything really."

"Well, that's good. You should come to the football game on Friday night," Elle suggests.

"Will you be there?" I ask.

The twins laugh. I must be missing some inside joke.

"Elle is a cheerleader, so yes, she'll be there," Peyton says.

"And you?" I ask, *curious about why her sister thought it was important to tell me that. Granted, I'm very thankful.*

"Peyton will be on the sidelines, coaching."

If I'm not mistaken, my eyes bug out of my head. "You coach football?"

Peyton shrugs. "I help out."

I nod. "Gotta say, that's really cool."

Peyton shies away from my compliment, but her sister doesn't allow it. Elle bumps Peyton on the shoulder and smiles brightly. These girls are the first twins I've met, and I can already see the closeness between them. On any given day, Brad and I are cordial with each other if we're not trying to fight one another.

The bell rings and I have no choice but to gather my stuff and head to class. Thankfully, Elle's locker is near mine, which gives me more time with her. Through the halls, everyone yells out her name, and guys stop and talk to her. It's awkward for me to stand there, but I don't want to leave. There's something about her that draws me in. I can't put my finger on it.

"Excuse me."

I shake my head. "I'm sorry, what did you say?" I ask the clerk.

"I asked where you'll be working?"

"Right, sorry. I'll be working in New York for a bit. I need some suits and business casual wear."

"Let me get your measurements, I'll be right back. In the meantime, take a look at our suits along the back wall." He points toward the back of the store before leaving me there. The last time anyone took my measurements was for prom, which seems so long ago. It's hard to believe I've been in the twins' life for over eight years.

The suits hang by color, starting with white and ending with jet-black. It makes me wonder if the coats come with a chart as to where they're supposed to go or if an employee here has a keen eye for the different hues and this is their task for the day. It's something I don't know if I'd have the patience for.

The clerk returns and ushers me into the dressing room where he has me stand on a pedestal. "Left or right?"

"I'm right-handed," I tell him.

"No, which way do you hang?"

"Um..."

He eyes my groin area and I let out a very uncomfortable cough.

"Our pants have a bit extra depending on which side you normally fall to."

How is this even a thing? All I can think right now is I'm thankful Elle isn't standing here with me. I don't know if I'd get over the sheer embarrassment. "Right," I say, although now that I'm thinking about it, I'm not entirely sure. I can honestly say I've never even paid attention.

My personal attendant goes to town, so to speak, with his yellow measuring tape, rattling off numbers to an assistant of his own, that I don't even remember entering the room. They both disappear, leaving me standing on the platform with mirrors all around me. I glance at myself, wondering what this guy sees. Does he see the stress and worry I have about my next adventure or the bags under my eyes from the lack of sleep I get each night? Every night since I accepted the offer, my mind races, filling my thoughts with dread and endless possibilities. Try as I might, I think about Elle and wonder what she's going to do during the time I'll be in New York. Will she miss me, call me and demand I tell her why I didn't share my news with her?

I'll be gone approximately ten weeks, living in an overpopulated city, working a nine to five job, three thousand miles away from the people I consider my family, with a three hour time difference. I'm excited, nervous and welcoming the opportunity to do something for myself. Every decision I've made since the day I met Elle, has been based on her. It's time for Benjamin Miller to expand his wings and see what else is out there in the world, and if doing so means Elle, and I are going our separate ways, so be it. It's probably time and honestly should've happened four years ago. California was never my dream. It's always been hers.

13

ELLE

With one last look at my final for this quarter, I make sure every T is crossed and every I is dotted. For the past week, I've crammed everything I could into my brain, knowing at best I walk away with a C-average. It's better than failing, and while it's still not up to par with what my parents want and expect, it's all I can give them right now, with the promise that I'll do better next quarter.

While I'm still upset with my dad for threatening to cut me off, he's right. I haven't been a model student or daughter as of late, and if I want a future, I need to figure things out. However, the future part has to wait because Peyton and I are heading to Aruba for spring break. As luck would have it, UCLA and Northwestern happened to vacation at the same time, a first for Peyton and I. I had asked to go to Cancun and the Florida Keys with my friends, but what I need is time with my sister. Besides, we can plan her wedding and focus on being sisters. For a while now, I've felt like our bond hasn't been as strong as it should be, and I miss it. I miss my sister.

I also miss my best friend. Ben's the guy who I've seen almost every day of my life since I was fourteen. He's also the guy who has conveniently disappeared, although that isn't entirely true, I have seen him, in passing, but he's clearly ignoring me. Deep down, I know it has to do with the night of his birthday. Whatever happened is my fault. The thing is, I don't know exactly what happened and he's not talking to me. A flippant wave as he's passing by doesn't really tell me anything. I want for him to pound on my apartment door, grab me by the shoulders and shake the crap out of me, all while yelling about how ridiculous I am for whatever I did. At least then, I'd know where I screwed up, and maybe I can try to fix it.

Although, something tells me there's no coming back from what happened between us. I think we crossed a line, one I never meant to cross. Ben knows for sure, and he's not saying anything, which leaves us in limbo. I have to do something to fix this... whatever this may be.

After another read through, I make a few changes to my paper, hoping I'm submitting the best quality work I can. I'm not naïve enough to think my efforts will be enough, but I'm hoping. My classmates start to turn their papers in, but I wait. I'm going to use every last second of the clock before I hand my final in. I have so much more to lose, by no fault of my own.

"Five minutes," the proctor says. I had hoped my professor would be here today or at least her assistant, but no such luck. Even if I wanted to sweet talk my way into a passing grade, I can't. The man standing at the front of the class with his eyes trained on each student doesn't give a hoot about who I am or my plight. Of course, my plight is my own. The administrator already took pity on me when Peyton had her accident. I don't have an excuse now.

Every minute, he announces the countdown. I feel like the song should play, and Rocky and Apollo Creed should start battling it out in the middle of the room. I try to focus on the words I wrote, tweaking and changing them around for better flow. When the test administrator declares one minute left, I save my document and send it to the classroom printer, where a small line has formed. Thankfully, I'm done. The stressing can happen while I'm on the beach, trying to piece my life back together.

As soon as I step out of the building, I tip my head back and let the sun shine down on me. Growing up, we'd come to California during vacations if the band wasn't touring. From the moment I landed here, I knew this is where I wanted to be. Making this decision wasn't easy, though. I thought about staying near Beaumont so that I could visit my father's grave, but with my mom and dad living here, it's where I wanted to be. Honestly, I don't know how Peyton does it, living in Chicago by herself. Although, since she and Noah have been together, he's living there as much as possible.

With Ben on my mind, I make my way over to the café where he has work-study. When he first got this job, I teased him only because he went from working at Whimsicality to the Java Spot, and had a slew of other jobs he could've applied for. He said working here made sense, it's what he knew and could easily do the job without much training. He was right, and this quickly became our hangout, except right now he's not here when he should be.

"Hey, Tim. Do you know where Ben is?"

He shakes his head. "Nah, he's not on the schedule today."

Odd. I smile. "Okay, thanks." It doesn't make sense that he wouldn't be here. He's always working at this time, but maybe he had a final scheduled. I pull out my phone and send him a text, and then scroll through the barely answered messages. When he does answer, it's one word, and usually, it's a yes or no, which is vastly different from a few weeks ago.

I try not to let it bother me as I head back home. Traffic is light, and when I get there, Peyton and Quinn are in the midst of a heated battle over whatever video game they're playing. They don't acknowledge me, and that's okay. This is something they share, although if you look at Quinn, you'd think he wouldn't be a sports fan. However, this is where his friendship with Noah comes into play. And probably Quinn's love for Peyton. While they bond over video games and sports, Quinn and I have our music. Well, more his than mine. I'm the least musically inclined one of the bunch, even though I can play the guitar.

"Let me know when it's safe to walk in front of the television." I stand there, waiting. I've been on the receiving end a time or two, getting yelled at because I walked in front of the TV at the wrong time. Over the years, I've learned to wait.

"You're clear," Quinn says. Instead of passing by, I drop my bag and take the spot in between them. Both lean toward me as if they know I need their comfort, but neither wanting to bring attention to the fact.

"Who's winning?"

"I am," Peyton says.

"She cheats."

Peyton throws her hands up in the air. "How, Quinn? We're playing on a console. It's impossible to cheat."

I look at Quinn, who shrugs. The game starts back up, and it's easy to tell who Peyton is. I start to laugh as she controls her future husband on the screen and when things don't go her way, she yells at him, almost as if he could hear her.

"Poor Noah. He's not even here to defend himself," I direct at Peyton. She rolls her eyes and continues her onslaught of Quinn, while I sit there, sandwiched in between my siblings.

When the game is over, Peyton jumps up and does a little cheer before sticking her hand out. "Pay up."

"You made a bet with her?" I look at Quinn.

"I've been practicing," he laments.

I point at Peyton. "And you don't think she has? Geesh, Quinn, she lives with a quarterback. I'm sure they play all the time."

"Noah loses too." Peyton is very nonchalant about beating Noah as she pockets the money from Quinn. "Go grab your stuff, Quinn will take us to the airport."

The beauty of having a private jet at our disposal is we don't have to book tickets. Our dad works with the pilot to file the flight plan, and the pilot tells us when to be at the landing strip. Last night, I packed everything I would need, which isn't much, and rush off to my room to grab my bag.

Peyton and Quinn are waiting for me, ready to leave. Outside, I stare at Ben's door, wondering if I should text him one more time or wait for him to respond. Maybe I need to step back and give him some space, even if it hurts me.

The drive to the airport takes longer than anticipated because of traffic, the only thing I hate about this area. You have to time your departure right, or you could get stuck for hours, all because someone put on their brakes at the wrong time.

When we finally arrive, we tell Quinn to have a fun week without us and thank him for dropping us off. The desk agent is laughing at us when we enter the facility. She tells us the pilot's waiting and to have a fun trip. The both of us run to the plane and climb the stairs. I come to a complete halt even with Peyton crashing into me.

"What gives," she says. "Oh."

"Yeah, oh." There are red and white roses spread everywhere and a bottle of champagne on the table. "You're so lucky."

"It's our first time really apart like this," Peyton says. I'm not even sure they're from Noah, but who else would do this.

"What about during the season?"

"He's home a couple of days a week, and I fly to him on Fridays."

"I see." Somehow, I knew this, but it didn't really register. Peyton and I sit across from each other and buckle up. Our flight attendant has notified the pilot that we're on board and ready and before I know it, we're off the ground and soaring toward paradise.

The stewardess pops the cork on the champagne for us and pours us each a glass. "Thank you," we both tell her. I reach across the table and tap my glass to my sister's. "Here's to a week of sun, sand, and whatever else we may do."

"Like plan my wedding, talk about boys and eat our way through Aruba."

I'm all for two of the three options she said, but talking about boys is something I don't want to do. As I look around the cabin, I realize Peyton is living most girls' fairy tales. I mean, what guy thinks about sending flowers ahead to decorate the inside of a plane? Noah does because he's crazy in love with my sister. I'm happy for her, beyond happy actually, but jealous all the same. I want what they have. I want the all-consuming type of love where we each know what the other is thinking or where we may be in a room full of people.

"I want what you and Noah have."

"What do you mean?" Peyton asks. I realize I hadn't meant to say that aloud, but now that I have, Peyton's looking at me expectantly.

"I want a guy who looks at me the way Noah looks at you. I want this"—I spread my arms out—"I want to walk in a room and search the crowd, only to feel my man coming behind me and when he touches me I know... I just know."

"You have all that."

"Pfft, with whom? I've never dated seriously since we

were allowed to date. It's not like my knight in shining armor is someone I know."

"But he is," she says.

"Who are you talking about?"

"Ben, of course."

"You've got to be kidding me, P. He's not even speaking to me right now, and I can guarantee you, we're not even close to being on the same page as you and Noah."

"Why do you think that?"

I sigh and down my flute of champagne. "I think I slept with him and I don't remember, and if I did, I might have been a total bitch to him the next morning."

"Oh, Elle." Peyton leaves her side of the plane and comes over to me, pulling me into her arms. I need this. I need to feel loved and worthy of someone else's affection, whether it's my sister or not. "We'll fix this," she whispers into my shoulder. I want to believe her, I do, but I fear Ben is too far gone, and I don't really blame him.

14

BEN

"*A*s I said in the ad and as you can see, the apartment is fully furnished." The woman who answered my sublet ad continues to look around. In her response, she stated she was looking for a short-term rental until her boyfriend returned from his deployment. What I'm offering is exactly what she needs.

"Are your neighbors quiet?" June asks. She reminds me a bit of Elle except with blonde hair. Although I have a feeling, everyone is going to remind me of Elle if I look hard enough.

"They are. I have no complaints." There's an older couple on one side, and Elle and Quinn on the other. If Quinn is serious about curbing Elle's partying, everything should be nice and quiet in this part of the complex. "There are a few college kids living here, but for the most part, they're very respectable. My friend sometimes has her friends over to use the pool, but no one around here really parties."

"Okay, that's good. I start my job on Monday as a nurse, so I'll have odd hours."

"You remember that I'll be back in ten weeks, right?"

"Yes," she says. "Randy, my boyfriend, will be back in about eight. I think I'll stay here and transition slowly into moving in with him."

"Perfect." There's an awkward silence that falls over us. June moves from room to room looking over everything she can, including the size of my closet. Thankfully, I cleaned before she came over. Otherwise she might find something unmentionable on the floor. I show her where to find sheets and towels, as well as how to use the washing machine even though it's probably pretty standard. "So, what do you think?" June is really my only hope. I didn't get as many inquiries as I thought I would, mostly because I didn't post the ad on campus. I didn't want Elle to see the ad and ask me what I'm doing. As it is, I've had a hard time ignoring her, but it's all for the best. At least, that's what I keep telling myself.

"I'll take it."

"Oh thank God," I say, exhaling loudly. "Sorry, I was just worried—"

"No, no, I get it. Believe me, you're helping me out too, so I think this will work perfectly. I have my stuff in the car, should I go get it?"

"Yeah, definitely. I'm just going to grab my things, and then the place is all yours." I hand her my spare set of keys and watch her walk out of my... well, now her, place. Once the door shuts, I relax a bit. The only thing left on my to-do list is to get on the plane and actually go to New

York. Most of my belongings have been packed for a few days, so now it's a matter of actually leaving.

Pulling out my phone, I send a quick text to my brother, letting him know I'm ready to leave. Brad said he'd hang out in the area and wait for me to call. It was his idea for him to take me to the airport. I think he volunteered because he's afraid I won't get on the plane. He's right because right now I'm second-guessing my decision. I know it's the right one to make, but making it is a whole other step.

June returns with an armful of her belongings. I realize I should be helping and immediately go to her and offer my assistance. "Here, let me help."

"I got this load."

"Is there more in your car?" Of course, there is, Ben! What a stupid question.

"Yes, it's the blue Beemer. Here are my keys." June slightly turns to the side. Her keys are dangling from her backside. I grab them quickly and rush out the door and down the stairs. Every few seconds, I look over my shoulder for Elle or Quinn, hoping I don't run into either of them. I've thought about telling Quinn, but I know he'll tell Elle and right now I can't deal with her reaction. It's best I leave and do my thing, consequences be damned.

Although, there shouldn't be any consequences. Elle should be happy for me. A true friend would encourage and congratulate someone in my position, and the fact that I think otherwise of Elle, proves we need a break from each other.

June's car is easy to find. I pile as much as I can into

my arms and head back upstairs. Inside, she has the curtains open, music playing and she's already making herself feel at home.

"Thank you, Ben. I promise to take care of your place while you're gone." June relieves my arms of her belongings, tossing them onto the couch.

"You're welcome. You have my number in case anything goes wrong, but it shouldn't. The management company has your information so there shouldn't be any problems there either."

"Perfect. Enjoy your trip."

I feel like I've just been kicked out of my apartment. I suppose in a sense I have. I nod, gather my stuff and walk out the door. I glance quickly at Elle's door, wondering if she's even home. As tempting as it is to knock, I don't.

My brother's waiting in the parking lot when I finally make it down the stairs and out of the complex. For whatever reason, it took me longer than normal. Maybe it's because I'm still hesitant about my decision or maybe it's because deep down, I want to say goodbye to Elle, to share my news, and know she's happy for me.

"Get in the car." Brad leans over the passenger seat and yells through the window. I do as he says, and no sooner do I shut the door, he's peeling out of the parking lot like he's being chased.

"Slow down."

"Buckle up."

Again, he's my big brother, and I do what he says, but he's laughing, and for the life of me I can't figure out why. "What's so funny?"

"You," he says.

"Do you want to explain yourself?"

Brad shakes his head. "The look on your face when you saw my car, I thought for sure you were going to run back upstairs and profess your love for Elle."

Sighing, I look out the window at the passing buildings and cars. "I thought about it, but no."

"You need this, Ben. You're better than the rest of us. You're going to make all of us proud."

"Thanks. Oh, by the way, I haven't told Mom yet. I thought I'd call her from the top of the Empire State Building or something like that. Do you think she'll want to come visit?" Once I left Beaumont and Brad followed, our mother sort of became a drifter. Not in the sense that she's not taking care of herself, but more so that if a job transfer was up for grabs, she'd sign up, and would take whatever. After awhile, you start to lose track of where your mother's living because she moves so much.

"Where is she these days?"

I shrug. "Delaware, maybe? Like I said, I'll call her when I get to New York." I would love to have the relationship Quinn, Elle, and Peyton have with their parents. I think Brad would too, but our mother has never been the type to stay in one spot. She gets bored and moves on. My father, while he made sure I had a college fund, has also been absent from my life. For the first few years he was around, but our relationship quickly became weekends, phone calls, and cards. When I entered high school, it was just cards. I suppose I could have a lot of resentment toward my parents, but I don't. They just weren't meant to be parents.

"Maybe I'll come out and see you." I look at Brad, who has his eyes trained on the highway.

"You should. I'd like it if you did."

Brad scoffs. "You say this now, but you're going to get there and forget all about Los Angeles. Some socialite is going to set her eyes on you, and you'll never come back here."

"I highly doubt it." Personally, I've had enough of the socialites.

"Maybe the girl next to you on the plane is a hottie, and you join the Mile High club."

I laugh. "The last time I was on a plane and had to use the bathroom, I hit my head on the ceiling because we hit some turbulence. I plan to stay firmly in my seat."

"A co-worker then. You'll meet someone, and you'll call me at the ass crack of dawn because you will have forgotten about the time difference, professing your love for whoever this woman is."

"And you'll mumble something I'll never be able to decipher."

"And the next thing I know, a wedding invite will be in the mail."

"Brad, you're sounding like a girlfriend I'm leaving behind."

He laughs and signals to get off the highway. Anxiety starts to build as the looming airport grows closer.

"Which airline?"

"United," I tell him quietly.

"You're doing the right thing, Ben. This will be good for you."

I hope. What if I get there and hate it? It's not like I

can leave and return to class. This quarter depends on this internship. If I screw up, graduation is in jeopardy. Brad finds a spot along the curb and pulls over. He hands me a white envelope.

"It's not much, but maybe it'll help. I did some research for you. There's a corner store two blocks from your apartment, and the laundry mat is across from the store. The subway is three blocks in the opposite direction. Don't splurge on anything unnecessary like Starbucks. Use the dollar menu whenever you can and eat ramen."

I clench the envelope tightly in my hand. "Thank you. You didn't have to." He really didn't, but I can't embarrass him by telling him I'll be paid while I'm there, plus I have the money from my work study and the stipend I get from my dad.

"Just be smart, Ben. Go out there and kick some ass."

"I will." We're not an affectionate family, but right now I don't care. I lean over the console and pull my brother into a hug. If it weren't for him, I wouldn't be going right now. I'm taking his advice and spreading my wings. Brad lets go, which is my signal to leave, and I get out of the car and grab my luggage. I don't wave goodbye or even watch him pull away from the curb. However, I do send him a text, **thank you**.

Inside the airport, once I'm checked in, I open the envelope. My brother has given me a couple of hundred dollars, money I know he doesn't have to spare, along with handwritten instructions on where everything is. As I read over his notes, tears prickle my eyes. I wipe them away quickly, not wanting anyone to see me crying or ask

117

if I'm okay because I am, and Brad has made it as such. This gesture, the thought he's put into making sure I'll be okay in New York, means more to me than I'll be able to tell him.

It's two hours of waiting before my flight is called. I'm at the back of the plane, in the middle with two men on either side of me, with a chair that doesn't recline. So much for joining the Mile High club on this flight, not that I ever would, but when Brad mentioned it, the thought did sound appealing. At least I'd have someone to talk to. The guy on my right is on his phone complaining about his wife, and the man on my left is already snoring. It's going to be a long flight, but worth it.

15

ELLE

*A*fter a long day at the beach, where Peyton and I laid under the cabana tent, watching families frolic in the sun, surf and build sand castles, we're finally getting down to the business of planning her wedding.

"Okay, I bought this and figured we can use this to keep track of everything. Most importantly, samples, notes, what you like and dislike can go in here. Plus, here are all the brochures from the list of venues we talked about."

Peyton slowly flips through the binder I created without saying anything. In fact, she's been very quiet each time I've brought up the wedding, opting instead to go out to dinner, hit the casino, take a dip in the pool or sit on the beach. I'm starting to think something's wrong and that the flowers Noah arranged for the plane were some sort of apology.

Without asking, I pull the notebook out from under her and close it, setting it aside. "What's going on?"

"Nothing," she states, turning her head slightly as if to indicate she doesn't understand.

"I call BS, P. You've been distracted since we arrived. We're on vacation. It's our last spring break together."

"And I'm enjoying myself."

I reach for my sister's hand and look at her adoringly. "Something's bothering you. I can tell. Are you pregnant?" Peyton's eyes widen. I smile, knowing I've uncovered her secret. "Eek, I'm going to be an auntie."

Peyton pulls her hands away and shakes her head. "Sorry to disappoint you. I'm not pregnant."

"Oh. Then what's wrong because I feel like you're not having fun."

"I am, Elle. But I have something to tell you."

I sit back in the booth and feel the blood drain from my face. "You broke up with Noah, didn't you? I mean, he sent all those flowers because he loves you, but..." My hand covers my mouth. "Oh God, is Dessie back? I'll kill her," I say without thinking my words through.

Peyton smiles and shakes her head rapidly. "Oh hell no. And no, Noah and I didn't break up, but we did decide to get married in Beaumont." Peyton's lips go into a fine line, and her eyes go wide. I let her news sink in, and while I'm upset, it's a decision she and Noah have to make. It's not my wedding.

"And you felt like you couldn't tell me this?"

My sister shrugs. "You've been so excited about everything I didn't want you to think I was ungrateful for all you've done so far. Getting married in Beaumont is something we feel very strongly about."

I scoot closer so I can hug my sister. "It's your

wedding, P. You can get married at the courthouse for all I care, just as long as you get married." Again, I'm speaking before I realize exactly what I'm saying. "What I'm saying is—"

"I know what you're saying. Believe me, when I say this, everything with Noah is amazing. I didn't know what happiness was until we finally got together. I mean, I always imagined what our lives would be like."

"And does your imagination serve real-life justice?"

"Not even close. I love him, Elle. Right now, our lives are complicated, but we both work so hard to make things easy. When he's in Chicago, he cooks and cleans so I can study, and when I'm in Portland, I do the same for him so he can focus on being the best quarterback in the league. We're both exhausted at the end of the day but when I curl up in his arms, I know I've made the right decision."

We hug again, and I fight back the happy tears I'm feeling. Seeing my sister so in love with the man of her dreams, fills me with hope. It gives me something to look forward to in the future. Not that there's a man on my horizon, but someday, I'm hoping there will be.

I open the binder and flip to the flower section. "What do you want to do about flowers?"

"Hydrangeas are a must."

"Yes, they are." I write a quick note. "Do you have a florist in mind?" I glance at my sister.

"Aunt Josie is going to do them."

"Oh."

"No, don't get the wrong idea. You and I are still picking everything out, but I figured it would be perfect for Whimsicality to do the flowers. They're going to cater as well."

"Aunt Josie has really turned her little flower shop into something amazing. I really miss it."

"Me too. Do you remember working there?" Peyton asks.

I nod. "It was some of the best times."

"The pay was horrible."

Peyton and I both start laughing. We were paid under the table, and by today's standards, the wage we were given would make our aunt look like a child laborer. However, none of us did it for money. We did it because we're family and once we were in high school, it became a weekend hotspot, unless you count the water tower.

"Do you remember when Ben broke the bucket of dishes?" Peyton asks. My brows lift, and my mouth drops open as the memory floods my mind.

"The band was on tour and Ben was insistent that he help out Quinn. Ben had the take-charge attitude and would go to the café every day after school whether Josie needed him or not."

"And she never turned him away."

Shaking my head, I think about how Ben was always around when our dad was gone. Even though Quinn was there, Ben always made sure my mom didn't need anything. Our mom, of course, loved having him around. Ben's always fit in with my family, sometimes more than I have. I think once my parents find out Ben and I aren't exactly on speaking terms, they'll side with him because my behavior has been atrocious. Ben has put up with far more than he should've and frankly, should've stopped talking to me months ago. But, Ben Miller would never do something like that. It's not in his nature so the fact that he has, really makes me wonder how badly I've screwed up. I wouldn't even know where to begin to fix things with him.

The gentle touch of my sister's hand on top of mine pulls me back to the present. "Where'd you go?" she asks.

"Just thinking about Ben," I tell her. I know they talk and part of me is desperate to ask her if she knows anything, while the other half of me feels she doesn't, or she would've said something by now. "Why don't you call him?"

"I have." I shrug. "My calls go to voicemail. When he answers my texts, they are one-word answers. I knock on his door, and there's no answer. I go to the café where he works, and he's not there. The last day I physically saw him was the Monday after his birthday. I don't see him on campus, checking his mail, leaving for school, and believe me, I've been watching. Lurking in the shadows, waiting to corner him and demand he tell me what's wrong."

"I wish I knew why he was acting like this."

I half smile at my sister and keep my eyes focused on the water glass in front of me. "I had a feeling if you knew something, you would've said, but I also didn't want to ask because I know you've both grown closer since your accident."

Peyton laughs. "I never told you this, but the day Noah came over to Mom and Dad's to confess everything and tell me he's not giving up on us, Kyle was there, and he tried to kiss me. When I told him I was in love with someone else, he asked if the guy was Ben. I told him no and he figured it out right after, but I started thinking, why not Ben?"

Peyton shakes her head at my shocked expression. "Not for me, but for you. And so I'm curious, E. Why not Ben? Because from what I can tell he loves you more than anything, and he has since the day he was adamant I was in his bio class. That boy followed me to the cafeteria, and once he laid eyes on you, he was a goner."

"Which makes no sense since we're identical."

Peyton shrugs. "We're different in our own ways. Besides, I was a tomboy, and you were the cheerleader. You attracted far more boys than I did."

"Only because every guy in school knew you were in love with Noah or they were afraid you'd show them up with your mad sports knowledge."

Our waiter appears and refills our water glasses. I take it upon myself to order us some dessert. I tell him we want something sweet, filled with caramel, hot fudge, and cake. There has to be cake. Peyton and I laugh when he asks if we plan to share. That's a definite no.

"Does Noah know who he's asking to be in the wedding?" I ask, determined to change the subject. As much as I'd love to rehash high school, those days are long gone. I can't get them back, not that I'd want to. Ben's birthday though, I'd love to go back to that night and not drink so much wine so I can remember what happened between us.

"I know he's made a list. He's having trouble deciding who he should ask as his best man."

"Really?" Although, he has a lot of close friends.

Peyton shakes her head. "Liam or Quinn."

"Wow. I thought for sure it'd be one of the guys from the team."

"I know. I was shocked. I thought he'd ask Alex, but Noah said that when he thinks of us standing up at the altar together, he feels as if it should be his dad or Quinn by his side."

"Well, this could be awkward. I mean, how am I supposed to hook up with the best man after the ceremony?" I ask teasingly. Peyton throws her napkin at me, in time for the waiter to appear with two monstrous sundaes. It's a mountain of ice cream sitting on top of chocolate cake with sauce drizzled over the top.

"Careful, the plate is hot," the waiter says as he slides them in front of our faces. My stomach turns, and my brain starts to get a cramp even before I've taken a bite. We tell him "thank you," and both look at each other.

"We each should've ordered something different."

"I know, P. I think this is a stomachache waiting to happen." I don't care though and dig in, taking my first big mouthful of the deliciousness in front of me. "Oh my," I say, covering my mouth. "This is so good." My words are jumbled and sound nothing like what I'm trying to say.

"Ssh, I'm busy." Peyton looks lost in dessert heaven. She closes her eyes with each bite she takes and moans. "I need to come here for my honeymoon."

"Where are you guys going?"

"We haven't decided yet. We've bought a few travel magazines to look for places, but ultimately, Noah's going to make the decision and surprise me."

"That's sweet."

"It is, and I don't mind as long as we're together." We let eating take over, neither of us talking until we've made a dent in the sundaes. "So about Ben?" Peyton leaves her question wide open, leaving it to my interpretation.

"The more I think about his birthday, the more I think we slept together, and if we did, I didn't treat him very well the next morning."

"Maybe you should ask him."

"I did. He said no, but I don't believe him. I think he's covering for me because I had been drinking. I remember arguing with him over something, and then nothing until I woke up."

Peyton sighs and sets down her spoon. I have a feeling I know what's coming. I sit up straight and ready myself for her lecture.

"I'm very proud of you. I know you've struggled since my accident, but it seems like you're trying hard to make a change. It hasn't gone unnoticed by me that you haven't had a drink since we arrived."

"I'm trying, P. I really am. Dad put a lot of things in perspective and this situation with Ben, it's because of something I've done. I have to fix it because not having Ben in my life isn't an option."

"He's your Noah," she says.

I look at her for a long minute before tears start to fall. Ben is my Noah, and it's taken me years to realize it. Maybe once it sinks in, I'll figure out a way to right my wrongs with him.

16

BEN

*D*espite having traveled many times with the James' family, I'm not prepared when I enter baggage claim and see a man standing there with my name on a sheet of paper. If it didn't say Benjamin Miller with the firm's logo on it, I probably would've continued to walk by and do my own thing.

"I'm Ben," I say to the man, sticking my hand out to shake his. He gives me a small smile and reaches for my hand, not to shake it, but to take my bag. In broken English, he tells me to follow him. I do, not because I need a ride, but because he has all my things on his push-cart and while I have a longer than normal stride, this man is weaving in and out of the New York airport popu-lation like his tail is on fire forcing me to jog to keep up.

The words sorry and excuse me are flying out of my mouth as quickly as the steps I'm taking. I bump, slam and sideswipe my fair share of people as I follow my driver. When he finally stops, I almost crash into his back. He turns and glares at me over his shoulder. I want to be like "what" but heed the advice of every online forum I read about New York, and keep to myself.

Once we're in the parking garage, this Mario Andretti walking version slows down and walks a normal pace. Maybe what I witnessed back there was a challenge between him and the other drivers as if they need to be the first ones out of the airport or they're being timed.

My driver doesn't ask where I need to go and I don't volunteer the information because frankly, I have no idea where I am. A major drawback of being in an unfamiliar city, I'm utterly lost. However, I'm excited to be here and get my feet wet, so to speak. One of the things my brother put in his note, was for me to explore. He listed places I need to check out, most of them within walking distance, and the ones that weren't, he gave me directions via the subway.

I pull out my phone and text him, letting him know I arrived. I leave out 'safely' because it's yet to be seen if I'll make it to my destination in one piece.

Brad: **Good, I'm glad. Have fun. Work hard. Meet a nice woman.**

The last part stings, but Brad's right. I don't know how to get over the feelings I have for Elle, but I need to try. It's not healthy for me to continue to pine for someone who isn't ever going to reciprocate my feelings. It's not fair to me, nor is it fair to ask her. In all the time I've known her, she's never indicated we are anything more than friends. This should've been my clue years ago.

After what seems like an eternity but in reality is

about thirty minutes, the driver pulls up in front of a building. He opens my door and rushes to the back to grab my luggage. I can't believe this is where I'll be living. The building is enormous and surrounded by others equally as tall with a few smaller ones mixed in. Honestly, this is a dream come true, a city high rise. I don't care if it's only for ten weeks. This is like something out of a television show.

The driver leaves my suitcase at my feet and is down the road before I can thank him. I watch everyone around me. Men and women of all ages move at a frantic pace. I used to think Los Angeles was fast, but I think New York is winning the foot race. A few people who are walking toward me veer off to their right and climb the wide concrete stairs leading to my apartment. For some odd reason, this makes me giddy. They're my neighbors or will at least be sharing an elevator ride with me.

I do the same after picking up my suitcase. All in all, it's about twenty steps until I'm opening one of the glass doors. There's a couple of men in dark suits sitting behind a massive desk. I approach them with a renewed confidence.

"Hi, I'm Benjamin Miller. I believe you should have the key to my apartment."

He presses the buttons on the keyboard and the lack of expression he had, has now morphed into confusion. "Mr. Miller, I'm not showing you as a tenant."

"One second." I slip my backpack off my shoulders and dig through the packet of papers Mr. Jacobs gave me before leaving. I hand him the slip, showing my address on there.

"I'm sorry, but you're in the wrong location."

"Oh?"

"Yes, see here..." He sets the paper down on this counter and shows me the address, which honestly means nothing to me. "You're about a twenty-minute subway ride away."

"But the driver brought me here, and I don't even know where here is. I just arrived from Los Angeles, and he was waiting for me and..." Panic starts to set in. What if the driver was at the airport for another Benjamin Miller? I mean, it's entirely possible. I do have a common name and mistakes happen, right?

While I'm in a full-blown freak-out, a woman approaches the desk and talks to one of the men sitting there. "Hi, I'm here to see Margie Smith with Omni, Inc."

"Wait, is Omni in this building?" I ask the man helping me. He nods and types something into the computer, and instantly he's grinning.

"Benjamin Miller, an intern with Margaret Smith?"

"Yes!" I glance to the gal next to me. "Thank you. You just saved my life." She smiles but says nothing. She's handed a badge and quickly disappears through the metal detector by the security gates. "Well, I'm thankful she said something."

"Me too, because I was starting to feel real sorry for ya." He places my badge on the counter. "This is tempo- rary until Omni issues you a permanent one. Take any of the elevators on the right-hand side."

"Thank you."

"Welcome to New York, Mr. Miller."

Towing my luggage behind me, I scan my badge and wait for the plastic windows to slide open so I can pass through. I'm sweating bullets right now, and my heart is beating unbelievably fast. For a second, I almost turned around and went back to the airport, giving in to my fear that I don't belong here, but it's stupid to feel that way. Omni's team chose me. I'm meant to be here.

The elevator ride is very short, but when I step off the elevator and turn toward the window, I see the tops of buildings. I walk over and look down and feel my throat drop. I don't know how high up I am now, but the cars on the street look like those little ones I used to play with when I was a kid.

Behind me, the glass front wall of Omni, Inc., is there, waiting for me. I press the button on the keypad and wait.

"May I help you?"

"I'm Ben Miller—" It's all I can get out before the door buzzes, and I'm able to step in, and that's when it hits me. The smell of success is all around. Five or six people are waiting on the leather sofas, and off to the right, staff are milling about. To the left, offices are overlooking the same view that I've just looked out over.

"Ben?" The woman behind the desk motions me forward.

"Hi, yes. I'm Ben."

"I'm Heather, you're early, but please follow me." I do as she says, following her down the hall. I'm not dressed appropriately for being here today and am wondering if I missed an email or something. I don't remember anyone saying I had to report for work today.

"Didn't feel comfortable leaving your luggage at your apartment?" Heather remarks. I look down at my suitcase and shake my head.

"The driver brought me straight here."

Heather sighs. "Of course he did. You can put your stuff here." She stops at a cubicle with three and a half gray fabric walls, a desk with some drawers, a computer, a phone, desk chair and a cabinet. "This will be your work-station."

I step in and set my stuff on the desk. As much as I'd love to sit at the computer and spin in the chair, Heather is waiting. I follow her down the hall, trying to pay attention, but the view is almost too much to pass up. I have a feeling I'm going to spend hours looking out the window and admiring the city from above.

"Margie, I have a wayward intern for you."

I half smile at Heather as I pass by. I don't like being labeled as a wayward thought. I've never missed an important date in my life, and I'm not about to start. I know my mind has been elsewhere, but I'm focused on this job.

"Mrs. Smith, it's a pleasure to meet you. Thank you for this opportunity."

"You too, Benjamin."

"Please, call me Ben," I say. I stand in her office, probably looking like a frightened schoolboy. I can't help but wonder what her view looks like, but walking behind her desk to look seems rather unprofessional.

"Would you like to have a seat?"

"Sure." I sit down in one of the chairs facing her desk. My hands grip the wooden armrests, and right now, I feel like I'm in the principal's office, about to get the scolding of my life.

"How was the flight from Los Angeles?"

"Long, hot, and a bit crowded."

"You would think with modern technology. We'd be able to make it from coast to coast a bit faster."

"I agree. I think Elon Musk will make it happen in our lifetime."

Margie smiles. "I imagine he will. You're going to be working side by side with Talia Roberts. You both start on Monday, and this is the project you're going to be working on." She passes me a thick blue folder with the name Eo on the front.

"As in the band?"

"Yes, you've heard of them?"

"A little. They don't get much airplay in Los Angeles."

Margie nods. "Which is exactly what you and Talia will change. Eo was nominated for eight Grammys and didn't win one. Their manager wants to change that. They have a new album coming out in early summer, and we want to deliver the best marketing campaign we can."

Oh, how I'd love to call Elle and tell her what I'm going to work on, but I can't. I won't. Knowing she'd be in the thick of planning with me does bring a smile to my face though and I know I can call Mr. HPJ and ask him for advice gives me the boost of confidence I've been missing.

"You seemed pleased with this project."

"I am. I have a few friends in the music business. I'm

assuming it's okay to bounce ideas off of them as long as I keep our client's privacy?"

"Of course, but remember, Talia is your partner. You both must agree on a marketing plan."

"I understand."

"Great, see you Monday."

"Thanks." I stand and carefully hold the folder upright so as to not spill the contents. "Oh, can you tell me how to get to the subway from here?" I ask before realizing Brad put them in my letter.

"Heather will be able to give you directions. Make sure you see her before you leave so she can take you to security."

"I will, thank you."

"Oh, and Ben," Margie says my name before I leave her office. I look at her expectantly. "Welcome to Omni. I have a feeling you're going to fit in rather nicely here."

"Thank you." I smile and turn toward my cubicle. This time, I do sit in the chair and take it for a spin. Might as well get this out of my system before I start work.

17

ELLE

*O*ur plane touches down and reality sets in. Our spring break should've been all about Peyton and her upcoming wedding, but it was spent trying to put my life back in order. Hard truths were said by my sister, a lot of tears shed, but in the end, Peyton has helped me see the error of my ways. I know I have an uphill challenge, not only with Ben but with my personal health as well.

As soon as the door opens, I follow Peyton down the stairs, almost falling when she starts screaming. I reach for her. However, she's gone before I realize what's happening. My hand goes to my forehead to shield the sun so I can see what's going on. Someone's waiting near the hangar who I assume is Noah. How Peyton knows it's him, is beyond me. Maybe it's the connection they share, the same type I want to have with Ben if he'll have me. If I were Ben, I'd run the other way after the way I've treated him.

When I reach the waiting car, Peyton pulls away from Noah. I stop and look at her, and that's when it hits me. She had a fantastic week in Aruba, but it's Noah who makes her unbelievably happy. Peyton has a different glow to her right now.

"Hey, Noah."

He approaches and hugs me. "Fun time?"

"Only the best with the James' sisters."

"Yeah, I know firsthand how fun you two are." Noah winks and takes my suitcase from me. I climb into the backseat, while Peyton takes the front. "So what's the plan?" I ask her.

"We're going to head to Mom and Dad's. Do you want to go?"

"Of course she does," Noah says as he starts the car. "Who doesn't want to go surfing with us after spending a week at the beach. Did you gals even go into the ocean?"

"Yes, we did. We went parasailing, scuba diving, and rented jet skis," Peyton says. She pinches Noah's cheek. Their cuteness should make me sick, but I want what they have. I want to be happy and in love. I want people to look at me and whomever I'm with, be it Ben or someone else, and roll their eyes and be jealous of the love we're sharing.

"So, what do you say?" Peyton asks.

The idea is tempting, but being at my parents keeps me from facing my demons unless I can somehow convince Ben to go. Maybe we need a weekend away so we can hash everything out. "No, I think I'm going to go home and see if I can corner Ben."

"You make Ben sound like a missing dog or something."

"Sometimes I feel like he is." Instead of engaging in more conversation, I look out the window and watch the passing scenery. Someday, I'm going to be a tourist and visit all the sites and do the tours of the movie studios. I want to see where the magic happens. I know everything there is about the music industry, but not the silver screen.

"Do you want to grab something to eat before I take you home?" Noah asks.

"No, thanks. I'm assuming Quinn did some grocery shopping while we were gone."

"Or had a massive party and your apartment is destroyed," Peyton adds.

I laugh. "Quinn and 'party' don't go hand in hand. He may have invited a lady friend over, but definitely no party."

"Does he have a girlfriend?" Peyton turns in her seat to look at me. "He never brings anyone to Mom and Dad's."

"I don't know. He doesn't bring anyone home."

"Huh." Peyton looks upset that I don't have the answer she's looking for. I know Quinn goes on dates, but he's never been serious about someone enough to bring her home to meet me, and if she's not meeting me, I can guarantee he's not bringing her to meet the rest of the family.

"I just want him to be happy," Peyton says. Noah places his hand on her leg.

"I'm sure he is, babe."

"Do you know something?" she asks her fiancé.

Noah shakes his head. "Nope, and even if I did, I wouldn't tell you."

"That's not fair. You're not supposed to keep secrets from me."

"Don't consider it a secret, P. Consider it as Noah protecting his best friend from the embarrassment Quinn's sisters are sure to show if he were to bring a girl home," I point out. The truth is, we'd probably gush over her, so I don't blame Quinn one bit.

"What your sister said, sweetie." Noah winks at Peyton, who giggles. Okay, now I'm about to be sick because their overly sweet and the mushy crap is too much. Thankfully, I'm going home because I don't know if I could take a two-hour car ride with them.

Noah offers to carry my bag up to my apartment, but I tell him I can do it. Peyton slides out of the car and pulls me into her arms. "I had the most amazing week," she says.

"Me too, P. We needed it." I hug her one more time. "Thanks for picking me up, Noah."

"Of course, Elle."

Waving goodbye, I rush toward my complex. There's a gathering going on at the pool. I pause long enough to see if Ben's there. He's not there, not that I really expected him to be. The door to my apartment is unlocked. Inside, Quinn is sitting in his chair, playing his guitar.

"Hey, how was your trip? I've been waiting for you to call."

"Sorry, Noah picked us up. I thought he would've let you know."

Quinn shakes his head.

"Sorry." I hear a door shut and it sounds like it's coming from Ben's apartment. "I'll be right back." It takes me under thirty seconds to get from my living room to Ben's front door. I knock, but the voice coming from the other side is female. My heart drops with the realization that I'm too late. He's been distant because he's met someone and didn't think he could tell me.

Back in my apartment, I shut the door and lean up against it. Quinn is staring at me, probably wondering if I'm about to have a breakdown. He doesn't know I've been sober since Ben's birthday. It's nothing I've broadcasted anywhere.

"Something wrong?" Quinn asks.

I shake my head, but quickly start to nod. "I think Ben has a girlfriend."

My brother looks at me, confusion all over his face.

"Did you know?" I ask.

Quinn strums his guitar before answering. "Honestly, I haven't seen Ben around for the last couple of weeks. Did you just meet her?"

"No, I left before either of them could answer the door." I push off the door and go over to the couch, flopping down. "Ben and I haven't exactly been talking as of late. I don't know why, but I was hoping to figure it out today." I leave out the part where I think Ben and I had sex. Quinn doesn't need those details about my life, and I don't need to see the disappointment on his face.

"I was wondering why he hasn't been over in awhile."

"I thought it was because he was studying for his finals. Guess not."

"Speaking of, how'd you do on yours?" Quinn asks. He sets his guitar down and leans back in the chair.

"I haven't looked yet."

Quinn motions toward my phone, which is sitting on our coffee table. I reach for it, scrolling through my app until I find the one that'll allow me to access my grades. It takes me a few times to type in my username, mostly because my fingers are shaking. I don't want to know if I failed any of my classes. I need four C's to pass. Any D's and I'll have to retake the class during the summer, which means I won't be able to graduate with my class.

"I can't." I hand my phone to Quinn and head into the kitchen to get something to drink. I'm not shocked when I open the refrigerator and find only bottled water and juices. Quinn has gotten rid of the beer he likes because the fridge is full of food, so I know either he or our mom had gone shopping. I actually wouldn't put it past our mom to drive up and take care of him while I was gone. From the day Quinn came into our lives, she's always had a soft spot for him. He's her baby boy despite her not being his biological mother.

"You failed," Quinn says loudly from the living room. Tears immediately fall, and my heart sinks. I did this. I put myself in a no-win situation and couldn't dig my way out of it. I tried, but not hard enough. I walk back into the living room, feeling as low as I possibly can and in need of a drink. I need something to numb the pain of being an epic failure. My dad is going to be so disappointed, and I don't know if it's worse knowing this or not walking with my class.

"Summer school it is."

Quinn hands me my phone with a smile. "You didn't fail. You passed, but barely."

"I did?" I choke out. The screen shows me C's with one C minus. "Why would you tell me I failed?"

"Because I wanted you to see and feel the letdown. I know you tried, but it was late. You're so much better than those grades, Elle. You know it. We all know it. Now you start this next quarter with a renewed outlook, and you kick ass with it. Shoot for the stars." Quinn comes over to me and holds his arms out. I push him away, but he doesn't budge. I don't care if he meant well, it was a dirty trick, and my heart hurts because of it. Quinn doesn't care and pulls me into his arms anyway, where I break down. It's not only my grades but Ben as well. I need him to give me a second chance, to right the wrong I've done to him. He doesn't deserve the way I've been treating him.

I also need him to come clean about the night of his birthday party. Something definitely happened between us, and he's not saying, and I know it's because of the way I reacted in the morning. I was confused and scared. Neither of which are adequate excuses for treating my best friend as if he's done something bad to me.

"Do you want to go grab dinner?" Quinn asks after he releases me. "I have a gig later at the coffee shop and could use a fan in the crowd."

"Sure. Let me go unpack and shower." I grab my suitcase and head to my room. Every piece of clothing from the trip heads right to the hamper, which is already full. Ugh, I have to spend tomorrow doing laundry, which is my least favorite activity. Thankfully, we have a washer and dryer in our apartment, so I don't have to lug my basket anywhere.

In the side pocket of my suitcase, I pull out the gift I brought home for Ben. Each time the tide went out, I combed the coastline for seashells, putting a few into a jar with some sand from the beach. I thought Ben would like this because the gift comes from my heart and not some tourist store.

I suppose I could give Ben the gift now, but don't want to screw up the relationship he's building. I don't know if he's told her about me or not. Not that I expect him to. Our BFF status is definitely on a hiatus.

For now, the jar will sit on my dresser, which will serve as a reminder of a well-needed break from reality and much-needed time with my sister.

18

BEN

*C*ollege is supposed to prepare you for long hours and late nights. One would think with the number of cram sessions and parties an average student takes part in we'd be prepared for the real world. This is not the case because of naps. We take naps, all the time. The only thing we're prepared for is the copious amounts of coffee we can drink to stay awake.

There are very few people left in the office this late at night. Most of us are interns, trying to earn a coveted spot with Omni, Inc. Each manager has two reporting to them, and it's the stiffest competition I've ever been in. Of course, Margie's team's going to win because I have music resources I can call upon to make sure our marketing proposal blows not only the clients and their manager but also the board out of the water. We need to knock the socks off everyone involved.

Right now, my partner, Talia, is face down on her desk. Over the past few days, I've found out a lot about her. She's from the midwest and is not a party girl, which has been evident with our late nights. By nine, she's always yawning, and by ten, she's usually out cold. Still, she's a hard worker and pulls her weight fairly. While I can stay up all hours of the night, she's a morning bird, always bright and cheery, ready to tackle the day. Honestly, I couldn't have asked for a better partner, and we make a pretty good team. We're like yin and yang, and we both want to succeed.

My only complaint, Talia is chatty. I know everything there is to know about her parents, brother, her roommate in college and the type of cows her grandparents raise on their ranch. Talia wears a size six shoe, which allows her to shop in both the adult and kids section.

Our first weekend in New York is coming up, and while I want to stay in and work, Talia and the other interns have made plans for us to all go out. As much as I'd love to say no, I can't. It'd be stupid not to build a network with the others. I don't want to be seen as someone who isn't a team player, both in and out of the office.

The security guard walks down the aisle-way, whistling. He does this to alert us to his presence to not scare anyone. Believe me, I've seen Die Hard a few times, and when I hear odd noises, I wonder what's lurking in the shadows.

"Mr. Miller, how are you this fine..." Bernard pauses and looks at his watch. "Morning."

"Morning, huh?" I glance over at Talia who is dead to the world. "I suppose I ought to wake her and get her home."

"You be safe out there," he says as he continues his patrol. New York is a somewhat safer city than it used to be, but it's still a city, and there's still crime all around us. It's really no different than Los Angeles. This is where I have the benefit over Talia. While I haven't been here before, I know what it's like to live in a city.

I close the file and pack it away into my bag before scooting across the aisle to tap Talia on the shoulder. "Talia, it's time to go." I like that she stays with me, even though she doesn't have to. I worry less knowing we're walking together instead of her out there at night by herself. I've grown a bit protective of her.

"I fell asleep, huh?"

"Yeah, but it's okay. I got a lot done. You can look it over in the morning. Well, later in the morning," I say as I look at my watch.

Talia stretches. "Maybe I should drink more coffee," she says, gathering her belongings.

"You're fine. I feel like we balance each other out."

"We do, don't we?" She slips her arm into mine, and we walk out together. There are a few more desk lights on, but we don't stop to see who else is working. If we stress about who's staying later than we are, our project will suffer. We need to have a clear mind at all times.

Talia and I walk to the subway. She stays close to me, keeping her bag between us. Her father gave her a list of things to watch out for, and how to not make yourself a target. I'd probably do the same thing if I were him. Talia also has to text him whenever she leaves her apartment or the office, as well as when she arrives at her destination. Her father seems a bit overbearing, but it's probably nice having someone who cares.

We make it to our platform just in time for the train. A minute later and we'd have to wait anywhere from fifteen to thirty minutes for the next one. That's the one drawback about working late. The cheaper transportation is hard to come by.

Talia takes the inside seat and leans her head on my shoulder. Even though we've only known each other for a few days, it's better than her leaning up against the dirty window.

When our stop is announced, I'm surprised to find Talia awake. Usually, she's out like a light once the train starts moving. Another reason she shouldn't ride alone at night. I've got to find a way to keep this girl awake in case I'm not around.

We only have a few blocks to walk once we get off the train. Talia and I live in a secured building, right across the hall from each other and on the third floor with no elevator. Talia thinks Margie and the other managers are trying to teach us a life lesson, showing us what we'll be able to afford if we were to win and be offered a job. I know she's right, and I honestly have no problem with my studio. It's quiet, I have a view of the street, which granted, isn't much, but it's different from L.A., and I need that right now.

After making sure Talia's in her place and her door's locked, I head into my apartment, locking the door behind me. My bathroom is immediately to the right, and after a quick shower, I'm crawling into bed after one a.m. I should go to sleep, but instead, I look at my phone. Elle's name is there, showing my most recent missed call. In fact, she's my only missed call. Each time, I either send her to voicemail or let it ring through, unable to bring myself to talk to her. I figure by now, she knows I'm gone and is probably wondering where the hell I am.

By accident, my finger touches her name, and the call goes through. I'm left with deciding to either hang up quickly and hope the call didn't register on her phone or to talk to her. It's late, and I need my sleep, but I take too long to decide, and she's saying hello.

My eyes close at the sound of her voice. I've missed hearing her, seeing her. "Hey." My voice is strained, and my throat feels as if it's going to close. This was a mistake. I should've held my stance and continued to ignore her. It's for my own good, even though I know she's freaking out. How do you tell someone you're in love with, you don't want to be near them because you can't be a part of their self-destruction? Never mind the fact that you can't bear to watch her be with another guy.

"Ben?" she says breathlessly, or at least that's what my imagination tells me.

"Hi, Elle." I want my words to be curt, but they're not. Another reason why I can't talk to her. My psyche doesn't allow me to be pissed at her.

"Where have you been? I haven't seen you around in weeks. You're not working at the café anymore. You never answer your phone, and I never see you on campus. I look for you all the time. It's like you've disappeared on me and I'm wondering if I need to send out a search party." Elle sniffles, a sure sign she's crying. I roll onto my back and close my eyes. The truth is on the tip of my tongue, but I've promised myself to keep my move a secret as long as possible. Elle will undoubtedly show up here, and right now I need to focus on my career and what's best for me.

"Elle..."

"No, I get it, Ben. I messed up, and I'd really like to talk to you about it, but you don't call me back, you barely answer my texts messages and when I go to your place... you have a girlfriend, and you didn't even tell me. I mean, I get it, but I want a chance to explain."

"There's nothing to explain, Elle."

"But there is. I know I did something and I think I have it figured out." Elle's definitely crying and I'm on the verge of telling her everything, starting with the fact that I don't have a girlfriend and the woman she can hear is only subletting. "Ben, please."

Hearing her plead almost does me in, but I can't do it. "Look, it's late, and I need to get some sleep."

"You called me back, Ben."

I sigh. I have a feeling I'm going to regret saying this. "It was by accident, Elle."

The intake of air is very audible over the phone. I have a feeling our friendship is over, despite what she's done, I've now hammered the nail into our coffin. "Ben?"

"I have to go, Elle."

"At least tell me her name so I can be cordial." No, I don't want you to be anything to June. I want you to continue believing she's my girlfriend and it breaks your heart.

"Talia. Her name's Talia, but she doesn't know about you, and I'd like to keep it that way."

There's a long pause before Elle answers, "I see."

"It's complicated, Elle. Right now, everything is just a mess and... I have to go." I hang up quickly and set my phone to Do Not Disturb. Knowing Elle the way I do, she'll end up drowning her sorrows in liquor and will start texting me all night. It's still early for her, and she's no doubt just getting started with the partying.

Never in a million years did I think her and I wouldn't be friends, and most of my life I imagined us together. What's worse, losing her means I've likely lost her whole family. I don't see myself hanging out with them or being invited to any of their gatherings. Mr. and Mrs. PJ have always treated me as part of the family, but only because I was an extension of Elle.

I make sure my alarm is set, and I roll over. As soon as I close my eyes, I see Elle sitting next to me in the uncomfortable waiting room chair while we wait for news on Peyton. I left Los Angeles to comfort her, to be there for her. I held her while she cried, turned my head when she'd disappear for hours, and made sure her family was taken care of. I did this because I'm so in love with her, it hurts. But not anymore.

The pain from loving Elle James stops now.

19

ELLE

"*That's* Ben's girlfriend?" Michelle says as she pulls down her sunglasses. A small pang of jealousy washes over me, knowing Talia is getting all the best parts of Ben right now, like his amazing sense of humor, his kind heart and how he always knows what I need. Well, I guess he knows what she needs now.

"Yeah."

"She's definitely out of college."

"I think she's a nurse. I'm not sure though. She definitely works in the hospital." It would figure Ben would date someone professional like a nurse or medical student, someone whose career is going to help people as opposed to what I want to do. I turn my attention back to my magazine, trying to dilute my mind with frivolous stories of the rich and famous, yet I can't seem to focus on what the Kardashians are up to these days because my sister's words keep replaying in my mind, Ben is my Noah. Peyton can see it, but I'm not sure I can or want to.

I don't want to ruin our friendship, even though I know the reason he's been so distant is because of the mistake I made. Losing Ben isn't an option for me.

"She's really pretty."

I know. I sigh. I've been spying on Talia since the night Ben, and I spoke on the phone. Oddly, I still haven't seen Ben either at home or on campus. I'd ask some of his classmates, but I don't know any of them, which only proves how selfish I've been where Ben's concerned. What type of friend only focuses on her own friends? Me. I'm that type of friend, and I disgust myself because of it.

"Do you want a hard seltzer?" Michelle reaches into her cooler and shows me the silver can with a mermaid on it. As much as I want to drink it, I shouldn't. I've been doing really well at staying sober, and I don't want to mess it up. There's a lot on the line for me right now, and alcohol doesn't help my decision making process.

"No thanks, I have water."

"What's with you? You haven't been out with us in weeks, and now you're drinking plain water when you could be drinking spiked water."

"It's our last quarter of school. I need to do well."

Michelle comes from money. I suppose I do as well, but not like her. Her family comes from old money. Not exactly sure, what that means but her father is a philanthropist and travels a lot. Her mother, according to Michelle, lunches. Which according to Michelle means her mom's screwing the pool boy. Her stories about her family make me so incredibly thankful for mine. Anyway, Michelle skates by at school because her family owns a building or something and no one wants to rock the boat, so to speak, on funding.

"Yeah, I guess," she says, but she still lifts the seltzer to her lips and takes a big drink. When these spiked seltzers came out, they were and still are all the rage. Low-calorie water with alcohol, what more could someone ask for. "Oh, here she comes. What do you think she's doing?"

I look up from my magazine to watch Talia come down the stairs. It looks like she's wearing a cover-up, which means she likely has her swimsuit on, which means... "Do you think she's coming in here?"

"Unless she's going to the beach, but traffic would be horrible at this time." Michelle looks at her wrist and laughs. I roll my eyes because she's not wearing a watch. "Where did Ben say he met her?"

"I didn't ask, and he hasn't been exactly forthcoming about her."

"But you're like besties."

Were. I don't bother to correct her. Right now, I don't know what Ben and I are. We're definitely not on the same speaking terms we've been on since high school. Nor is he sharing information about his new love. I always thought that when Ben finally decided to settle down, he'd introduce her to me so we could be friends. It's pretty clear Ben's been dating Talia for some time because she's living in his apartment. Have I been so lost in my own head that I didn't even notice her around?

No, none of this makes sense. As much as I want to deny it, I'm certain something happened between us on the night of his birthday and if that's the case, where was

Talia? Would Ben cheat? No, I don't think he would because he's so loyal, so none of this makes sense. Ben isn't the type of guy who moves fast, so where did Talia come from?

"I'm going to go talk to her." Tossing my magazine down, I stand. Michelle does too, except she places her hands on my shoulders.

"And say what?"

I look over her shoulder, toward the area where Talia disappeared and sigh. "I don't know, but something is off."

"Maybe, but Ben obviously likes her, and you have to accept that."

Tears prickle my eyes. I'm not even sure why I'm so emotional about this. I don't want to believe my sister is right, and that Ben is the one for me. He's always been my best friend, the one I've turned to for everything. I've had the best of both worlds, having Ben and Peyton by my side, talking about school, life and... guys.

Ben has always been my go-to about guys, asking him ridiculous questions on whether so and so likes me or if I should date someone, and yet at every major rite of passage, Ben and I went together.

"Do you think... never mind." I turn and gather my stuff. There's one question on my mind and only one person who can answer it. That's if he'll even talk to me.

❧

THE DRIVEWAY to Brad's new place is about a half mile long, winding through dense forest until the land opens up to a wide area with a gorgeous mansion. Behind the main house is a bungalow where Brad stays while working on the owner's cars.

Parking in front of the garage, the sound of machinery fills the air. When the noise stops, music takes over. I walk in and look around for any sign of Brad, but see none.

"Under here," a voice calls out. I walk around the car, looking at the ground, wondering if he's under there. In the front, legs stick out, and I laugh at the sight.

"Brad?"

"Yep." Before I can say anything else, he pulls himself out from underneath. There's a smile on his face, but it quickly morphs into a grimace. Brad and I haven't exactly been friends over the years, and even though Ben has told me otherwise, I feel as if Brad resents me because Ben moved here. "I don't service other vehicles." He tries to go back under the car, but I grab his pant leg to hold him still.

"I'm not here for a car repair."

"So why would you come all the way out to the canyon?"

"Because of Ben."

Brad pushes himself back out. "What about him?"

"I was hoping you could tell me what's going on."

He shakes his head. "Don't know what you're talking about."

"Really?" I ask, putting my hands on my hips. "Because one minute we're best friends and the next, he's avoiding me and dating some girl named Talia who has already moved into this apartment."

Brad smiles and continues to shake his head, which I find annoying.

"You know something."

"No, I don't. What I do know is you need to let him go. Release this imaginary hold you have on my brother so he can live his own life and not the one you have mapped out for him."

"What're you talking about? Ben does his own thing."

He smirks. "Ben does no such thing. He didn't even want to move out here, but he did because of you."

"He didn't have to."

Brad laughs once. "Really? Because the constant whining about how you don't want to be alone, even though you have your brother here, not to mention the fact your family are not far away, wasn't a plea with Ben to apply to UCLA? A college, mind you, that he didn't even want to attend."

"I don't whine, and Ben could've made his own decision."

Brad stands and picks up the rag on the car to clean his hands. "You don't get it, do you?"

"Get what, exactly? You are talking in spades, Brad. I'm here because I want to know what's going on with Ben or better yet, where he is. Because he's not at school, he quit his work study, and I never see him at the apartment."

He throws the rag down onto the counter and looks at me. "Since the day Ben met you, his life has been about Elle James. Elle, this. Elle, that. Your family adopted him as if he were some stray animal you found on the street corner."

"Are you jealous because Ben went on family vacations with us? Is that the problem? Because I don't understand, Brad. Shouldn't you be happy for your brother that he had some worldly experiences in his life? I'm sorry, we didn't invite you, but you and I aren't exactly friends."

"No, we're not, which means you should leave."

"I'm not leaving until you tell me what's going on with Ben."

Brad turns his back on me. "You need to leave Ben alone, let him live his life. For eight years or so, he's been under your spell, and it's time he figured out who he is. He's never been given a chance to be Benjamin Miller because he's always been Elle's best friend. For once, Ben's putting himself first. I wish I could say I'm sorry, but I'm not. It's about time he's removed himself from your clutches."

"My clutches? You make me sound like I've done him a disservice by being his friend, and yet Ben's had opportunities he would've never gotten. How easily you forget it was Ben, who came up to me and followed me around. I could've ignored him, treated him like crap, but I didn't because he made me laugh because he saw me for me and not who my family is." I wipe angrily at my tears. "All I'm asking is for you to tell where he is. There are things I need to say to him that can only be done in person."

Brad faces me and slowly shakes his head before shrugging. "Sorry, don't know."

"You're a liar Brad Miller."

"No, I'm a big, brother protecting his little brother from the big bad wolf." He tilts his head toward the door. "I think it's time for you to go now. I'm sure Daddy's credit card hasn't been used in the last hour, better hurry before it burns a hole in your pocket."

I flip him off because I'm too angry to get the words out. However, my action doesn't even faze him. He waves goodbye, leaving me no choice but to leave. Once I'm at the bottom of the driveway, I pull over and let my tears flow. I wasted half a day thinking Brad would help me. I'm left with no other choice but to ask Talia, plead my case with her while making sure she understands I'm not a threat to her relationship with Ben.

The question is, when I finally confront him, what will I say? Do I demand he tell me about the night of his birthday? What if he doesn't, where does that leave us? Deep down, I feel as if something happened between us, something triggered this avalanche of weirdness and I need to know what so I can fix it. Brad's right, in a sense. For eight years, Ben and I have been friends, and I'm not about to let our relationship end. With or without Brad's help.

20

BEN

I love New York City. Okay, love may be stretching it, but I'm definitely happy and glad I decided to take the internship. My workload has increased. Never a bad thing when you're trying to impress your boss. At our weekly check-in, Margie was ecstatic with what Talia and I had put together for Eo's management team, which was basically starting the group at the bottom by rebuilding and expanding their fan base with a series of summer concerts. It was a shot in the dark, but one Talia and I were happy to present. We still have a lot of work to do on our proposal until it's finalized. However, Margie wanted to see how we handle individual projects as well. I can say, without a doubt, I'm enjoying this job.

Tonight, Talia and I, along with two other sets of interns are going out for drinks to unwind from the long work hours we've endured as a result of our managers including us in their meetings. Coming into this internship, I didn't know what to expect. Professor Jacobs didn't have a lot of information on what my duties would be, other than I'd be working in the field of marketing. Being included in the day-to-day dealings has been a dream come true for me.

The bar we're in is one of the new trendy hot spots with music so loud you can barely hear the person next to you. Yet, we continue to yell at each other, we nod like we understand what the other person is saying, and we laugh when they laugh because we don't want to embarrass ourselves and miss a social cue.

Tara orders a round of shots. She, along with Ashley, Roy and Jeff are the other interns working for Omni. Everyone, including Talia, thinks we're long overdue for a night of debauchery. I don't disagree, but I've been down this road before and getting sloppy faced drunk usually leads to bad choices, which leads to life changing moments.

Okay, not all parties end up like my birthday. That night was nothing more than an unfortunate incident. One I'd love to forget, but can't. It doesn't matter how hard I try, Elle is always at the forefront of my mind. Maybe it's because my project revolves around a band and I spent so much time with 4225 West, that it's bound to bring back memories. I remember my first tour with them. I didn't think my mom would let me go, but she shocked everyone when she told me to have fun.

"Okay, I've cleaned the house, and I bought her flowers."

"I'm sure she'll say yes. Do you want my dad to come over?" Elle asks. She's currently sitting on my couch with

her knees pulled to her chest, reading one of the books that's on our required summer reading list. I have yet to start mine, while she's on her third.

"I think my mom would crap her pants if Harrison James was in her living room."

Elle looks up from her book and rolls her eyes. "He can be very smooth when he wants something."

"And he wants me to come on this month-long tour?"

She shrugs. "His princess does."

"You're so spoiled."

Elle closes the book and sets it down on top of her bag. "I'm not, Ben. You've been to my house. We live modestly. We have chores. We work." By we, she's referring to her brother and sister. Yes, she's right. I've never known children of famous people who have jobs, albeit, they work at the café which is owned by family. However, the Powell-James siblings stay out of trouble and are never in the tabloids. Believe me, I've Googled Elle far too many times.

"You're right, I'm sorry. Maybe your dad should come over or your mom."

Elle digs through her bag and pulls out her cell phone. She types away but doesn't tell me to who. The nerves I was feeling a few minutes ago have increased tenfold. I've never had someone famous in my house before, and I'm not sure how my mom will react. I know she loves the band and was a fan long before we moved here. Me choosing to fall for Elle, was just dumb luck.

I begin to pace, and when I'm not pacing, I'm sweeping the floor and wiping imaginary dust particles off the lampshade. Elle tells me to stop worrying, but I can't.

The sound of a motorcycle rumbles to a stop in front of my house.

"You texted your dad?"

She shrugs. "Like I said, he's smooth."

"Crap on a cracker." Since meeting Elle, I've tried to clean my mouth up. For the most part, my mom lets my brother and I get away with anything, including our language. However, Elle said she didn't like it, so I've tried to watch what I say, at least when I'm around her.

I jump at the sound of Harrison's knuckles hitting my door, even though I knew he was going to knock.

"Stop worrying, everything will be fine," Elle says as she goes to open the door for her dad. "Hi, Daddy."

"Hi, princess." He kisses the top of her forehead, and that's when his eyes meet mine. "Ben."

"Hello, Mr. HPJ." Elle's parents have ridiculous long last names.

"Please, call me Harrison or Elle's dad."

I shake my head. I refuse, and honestly don't know why. I've known Elle and her family for almost a year now and I still get nervous around them.

"Daddy, come sit. Ben's mom will be home any minute." Harrison follows Elle into the living room. He's dressed the same as always with his khaki shorts, distressed shirt, and beanie. Not to mention, combat boots.

No sooner do they sit down does my mom walk through the door. "Benjamin, what on earth is wrong, you look like you've seen a ghost."

I swallow hard and try to smile. "I'm fine." My head turns toward the couch where Harrison and Elle are sitting.

"Oh my is that..." My mom starts fussing with her hair and quickly pulls out her phone. It looks like she's about to take a selfie, but I know she's checking to make sure she looks presentable. "You could've warned me."

"He literally just walked in the door."

"Hello, Mr. Powell-James. So nice of you to come to our home."

Harrison stands and extends his hand. I glance at Elle, who doesn't seem to have a care in the world. "Happy to be here, Brenda. It seems the children have asked that I come to ask you an important question."

"Oh?"

"Elle would like Ben to accompany us on our summer tour. It'll only run for a month in the US, and we'll travel by bus."

"Oh." My mom looks from Harrison to me and then back to Harrison. "I don't know. I thought you were going to work this summer, Benjamin."

"I am. I will."

"Ben will be part of the road crew, so he'll get paid while we're gone."

"And he'll be responsible for his own stuff?"

"No, he won't, Mrs. Miller. Despite what my daddy might say, my mom would never allow it," Elle stands and chimes in. "Can he please go? We won't get into any trouble. My parents will know where we are at all times. And anytime you want to come to one of the shows, you just tell me, and we'll make it happen."

I expect Harrison to chastise Elle for speaking over him, but he doesn't. He smiles and puts his arm around her.

"Elle's right. Ben will be treated like family."

My mom looks at me. I can see the wheels turning in her brain. Every few seconds she sighs, making me wonder if I should ask Elle to leave so my mom and I can discuss the offer on the table.

"Have a good time, Ben."

"YES!" Elle screams and wraps her arms around me. "We're going to have the best summer. Thank you, Mrs. Miller."

"You're welcome, Elle."

"Thanks, Mom, and Mr. HPJ."

"You're welcome, Ben. I'm glad you're coming on tour with us."

"Me, too."

That summer I expected things to change between Elle and I. We were alone so many times on the bus, but the friendship wall was up, and it was too tall for me to climb. I'm not sure a ladder would've helped. After that, I sort of went with the flow and followed her lead, until it ended us up in my bed and our friendship severely damaged. Hindsight is fifty-fifty. I should've told her no.

The warm feel of a hand pressed into mine brings my thoughts back to the present. I look down to find Talia, smiling up at me with dreamy eyes. It would be so easy to kiss her right now or even when I stop outside her door later, but emotions mess everything up. Instead of letting go of her hand, I hold on a bit tighter until our round of drinks show up, and I have no choice but to let go.

We each grab a shot glass and hold them high in the air. "To the most amazing set of interns who are going to take New York by storm!" Ashley shouts. Our hands meet in the middle and liquor splashes everywhere, some slipping down my arm. I'm a little annoyed at the mess, but I can't let it bother me. Not right now, not in front of my peers.

The liquor goes down easy, way too easy for my liking. I order the next round almost immediately. I know my limits, but sometimes it's nice to forget, and this might be one of those times.

I lose count of how many rounds we end up drinking, although I'm pretty sure I bought two. On our way home, my arm is around Talia and hers is hanging onto my belt loop. We're closer than we should be right now, but I like it. I like feeling the heat from her body and the reverberations of her laughter.

The six of us decide to stop for pizza. It's a necessity in the city, and the little mom and pop places that you pass by have the best pizza. Inside, the standing room only parlor is warm. The older lady behind the counter serves each of us a slice. At a dollar, you can't go wrong, and after all the alcohol we've had, we need it.

The girls are laughing. At what, I have no idea. Talia keeps falling into me, and when I'm not eating my pizza, my hands are on her hips, holding her steady. She put away more booze than I thought she could and I'm hoping tomorrow isn't a bummer of a day for her. Thankfully, we're ahead on our project so we can take a day off.

Ashley and Roy want to hit another bar, but after another slice of pizza, I'm ready to head home. "I'm going to head home," I tell Talia. She sets her hand on my chest and looks into my eyes. I can't read her, not like I can

Elle. I close my eyes and will any thought of Elle away. "Are you going to stay?"

She shakes her head slightly. "No, I think I'm going to go home with you."

We tell the group we're leaving, and we'll meet up with them Sunday morning for coffee. Outside, we go our separate ways, with Talia and I heading toward the subway, and again, my arm is around her and she's leaning into me. Part of me is tempted to see how we fit together, but I'm not in favor of rocking the boat or sleeping with a co-worker.

In a few weeks though, she may not be a co-worker. There's nothing saying we'll win the competition, and if we do, if both of us take the job. However, it would be nice to be with someone who cares for me... as long as she's not drunk.

21

ELLE

*I*t's true, Brad Miller and I haven't been the best of friends. Sure, we both could say we haven't been friends at all. Back in high school, the rumor was Brad had a crush on me. For a brief moment, I had given him some thought because he was the leather-wearing motorcycle-riding bad boy that every girl dreams of. My dream lasted a whole two minutes or so. As hot as he was, and let's be honest, still is, because the Miller men have amazing genes, he wasn't the one for me. As odd as it sounds, I didn't like the way he spoke to me or other girls, for that matter, always putting us down and acting like he was better than the rest of us. The bad boy image has always been alive in our home, and I can't imagine my dad saying anything rude to my mom.

And maybe that's why Brad hates me and is trying to keep me away from Ben. I don't know for sure, but it makes sense, at least to me. What I do know is Ben's hiding something. Granted, we both have secrets.

Everyone does. And lately, I've probably kept my fair share of things from him. Looking at my current situation, this is the cruelest form of payback. Ben is essentially being me, which is really uncharacteristic of the man I know and grew up with. He's always been the type to wear his heart on his sleeve, and making sure I know exactly what he's thinking. Of course, over the years, I've been able to read him like an open book, but since his birthday... well, everything's changed since that night.

Which, is why I'm standing in front of a plate glass door with my hand on the brass door handle, willing myself to push down on the lever so I can open it. The word hypnotherapist keeps my feet grounded on the sidewalk and my thumb from pressing down to release the lock keeping the door shut. After hours of research on how to relive memories, I found Dr. Sanders, who seems to have a five-star rating on every review site, with accolades of how she's helped people recover lost and suppressed memories.

Truth be told, I'm scared. I'm afraid to find out I've done something horrible to Ben, even though deep down I know I have. There's a reason I don't remember the night of his birthday, and today I'm hoping to find out what that is.

With a deep sigh, I muster up the courage to open the door and step in. The hallway is drab and dark with hardwood floors that slope. My flip-flops smack loudly through the corridor. I expected this building to be bustling with people coming and going. Not quiet and void of life.

At the end of the hall is where I find Dr. Sanders'

office. While my nerves may be getting the better of me, I don't hesitate to twist the doorknob and enter. The office is warm and inviting with its muted blue walls and plush beige carpet. The receptionist smiles at me. "You must be Elle." She stands and holds out a clipboard.

"Yes, I am."

"Please fill this out. Dr. Sanders will be with you momentarily."

Taking a seat, I look over the attached papers. All the questions are common: name, address, and person to contact in case of an emergency. It's when I get to the question asking me why I'm here, my hand stalls and my mind starts to race. Do I put the reason? Do I tell the receptionist that I screwed up and I need to find what's going on?

The door of what I'm assuming is Dr. Sanders' office opens, saving me from having to fill out the loaded question. I stand and meet her halfway.

"Elle, why don't you come right in," Dr. Sanders says, motioning toward her office. Inside, the walls are a darker blue, and I already find myself at ease. Can the color of a room really make someone feel differently? "You can sit on the couch."

I do as she suggests and immediately sink into the plush cushions. I could easily see myself taking a nap here, and it makes me wonder if Dr. Sanders snuggles up in between clients.

"Before we get into the reason you're here, let's talk about you for a minute. Tell me about yourself."

"I'm nervous."

"I understand, but there's nothing to be nervous

about. We're going to talk, and I'm going to try and help you."

"Okay," I say with a deep breath. "Well, I'm an identical twin, a senior at UCLA and last winter my sister was almost killed in an auto accident. Since then, I haven't been the same. When my sister and I were five, a drunk driver crashed into our father's truck, and he died, and his accident was very similar to Peyton's – that's my sister. Our mother sort of remarried a little over a year after my father's accident. As of late, I haven't made the best decisions, and I fear I've done something to hurt my best friend, which is why I'm here."

"What do you mean your mom 'sort of remarried'?"

"My parents aren't married, at least not on paper."

"They have a common law marriage."

I nod.

"And your stepfather, do you like him?"

"I love him. He's our dad in every sense of the word, and honestly the only father figure we know besides our uncles. My sister and I don't remember our father, only with pictures and stories we've been told. My problems don't stem from a bad home or anything of that nature. When my sister almost died, I did too. It's a twin thing," I say, shrugging. "And while she's doing really well, I haven't recovered."

"Tell me about your best friend."

I do, telling her everything about Ben from the day we met to our last phone call. I share every detail about our friendship, from our study sessions, family vacations, and how he's been my rock for as long as I can remember.

"So why are you here?"

I clear my throat and rub my now sweaty palms over my shorts. "Ben's birthday was a few weeks back, and since that night, things have been strained between us," I pause and try to gather my thoughts. "I woke up in his bed, naked. We both were. Ben tells me nothing happened, but I don't believe him."

Dr. Sanders adjusts in her chair. The yellow notepad she's been scribbling in, wobbles on her crossed leg. "Do you think Ben raped you?"

My mouth drops open, and I shake my head. "No, not at all. Ben... he wouldn't do that. He's my best friend or was until his birthday."

"I've seen many cases where one party considered the other a best friend, only to have the unthinkable happen."

I shake my head vigorously. "Not Ben. He would never do anything to hurt me." This, I'm sure of. We may not be on the best terms now, but that's because I messed up, not him. There's no way Ben would ever take advantage of me. It's not in his nature.

"The reason I asked is that often people repress traumatic memories. If you were to have an unwanted sexual encounter with the man you consider your best friend, coupled with the stress of your sister's accident, your mind could've blocked it out. Do you remember if you fell down the day of Ben's birthday or if you hit your head on anything? What about drugs?"

Again, I shake my head. "I don't remember hitting my head on anything. As far as drugs..." I shrug. "I've taken pills in the past, you know to numb everything, but I don't remember if I did the night of Ben's birthday. I was drinking though. I remember a girl flirting with him, and it bothered me. I don't know why because it never has before. And lately, I've been lost. At least, that's what my family and Ben say. I've partied a bit too much, let my grades slip and haven't been the person people know me to be."

"And who's that?"

I sink deeper into the couch, pulling my leg up under my other one and rest my elbow on the armrest. My head falls easily into the palm of my hand. I don't know if it's because it's so warm in here or if it's because Dr. Sanders has a soothing voice, but I find myself wanting to open up to her. I guess she's good at her job, otherwise I can't imagine speaking freely.

"I used to be this sweet and fun-loving girl who cared about her friends, her grades and what people thought of her. My family always came first. My image was important. I wanted to excel at everything I did."

"And the accident with your sister changed all of this?"

"Yeah, it did. The doctors said she was going to die and there wasn't anything I could've done to help her. I felt this... ache deep inside, and even though she healed, my ache never went away, so I started drinking to numb the feelings."

"And where was Ben through all of this?"

"By my side. He came out to Chicago, where the accident was, and stayed until the hospital discharged my sister. He even spent the night with her so she wasn't alone. He helped my family, so they didn't have to leave Peyton's side, making sure there was always fresh coffee, food and anything they needed readily available. And he held me when a wave of emotions would take over. He let me cry on his shoulder." Tears start to fall, and I find myself wondering if they're for Peyton or Ben because right now, reciting how Ben was with my family during Peyton's accident has me asking why I've never given him a chance. His actions far exceeded what a best friend would do for someone. Peyton's right, Ben deserves more from me. However, the question is, can I give it to him? More importantly, will he even accept anything from me?

"I want you to lie back and close your eyes for me, Elle. I'm going to put you under and see if your subconscious remembers the night you're missing. I want you to listen to my voice and try to relax your body. If at any time you're uncomfortable, I want you to raise your hand, and we'll stop. Okay?" Her voice has changed, the tempo is slower, and she's quieter than before.

"Okay," I say.

I do as Dr. Sanders instructs. Soft music starts to play, and I can sense her walking around the room. Even though my eyes are closed, I feel as if the room has become darker. I'm tempted to peek, but don't want to open my eyes and find her hovering over me.

"Breathe in and out, Elle. Let everything go. Let your body mold into the couch and set your mind free. Where's your happy place?"

"The beach."

"Let's go there. What do you see?"

"My dad, brother, and Ben."

"What are they doing?"

"Everyone's surfing, except for Ben. He's... looking around."

"Do you think he's looking for you?"

"No, he's mad at me."

"Why's Ben mad, Elle?"

"I hurt him."

"Do you know what you did?"

"Yes."

"Does Ben want to talk to you?"

"No, he keeps walking away."

"Why is that?"

"Because I hurt him."

"What did you do, Elle?"

"I kissed him."

"Did he push you away?"

"Yes, he did, but I kissed him again and again. We fought. He asked me if I'm sure."

"What did you tell him?"

"Yes."

"What happened that night, Elle? Why is Ben upset with you?"

"Because we had..."

My arm goes up. I'm not sure if it's instinctual or not, but I'm angry. Not only at myself, but also at the fact that I'm awake. "Put me back under."

Dr. Sanders shakes her head. "I think you have your answer."

"But what if I don't?"

"What do you remember, Elle?"

I rub my face, pushing away the uneasiness I feel. "Ben and I..." I have trouble forming the sentence that has damaged our relationship. "We crossed the line."

"Is his pain from the act?" she asks.

Shaking my head, I wipe away the tears streaming down my face as the memories of that night come flooding back. "I hurt him," I choke out. "I shunned him when I woke up, and he lied to me."

"Why do you think he lied?"

"To protect me?" I question, but she doesn't have the answer, only Ben does, which means I need to find him so we can hash things out once and for all.

Dr. Sanders hands me a few tissues and gives me a moment to collect my thoughts. "Do you feel as if you have your answer?"

I nod.

"How about another appointment? Not for hypnosis, but to talk. I'd like to help you find your path again."

Again, I nod. "I'd like that. Right now, I feel more lost than ever." She reaches for my hand and gives it a reassuring squeeze. "Why did I block this out?"

Dr. Sanders crosses her legs. "Our psyche is delicate. Without more knowledge of who you are, I'm guessing you didn't want to ruin your relationship with Ben, and you knew it would. It did. Your mind shut down and did the only thing it knew to do, erased what could potentially change your life."

"And in the process, Ben distanced himself from me."

She uncrosses her legs and leans forward. "Without knowing Ben, my guess is he feels something for you, and your rejection of him was the door slamming in his face. The only way to find out is to speak to him."

I shrug. "That's just it. I can't find him."

AFTER THERAPY, I drive to parents. When I pull into their driveway, the garage is open and my dad's bike is gone. I shouldn't be surprised. It's gorgeous out and my parents like to go for rides. Still, I park and head inside, shocked to find my mom sitting on the couch. As soon as we make eye contact, tears begin to stream down my face.

"Elle, what's wrong?" she asks, getting up and rushing over to me. I'm in her arms, being cradled against her chest, before I can even mutter a single word. "Ssh, it's okay."

"But it's not, Mom."

My mom continues to hold me, swaying back and forth, while humming the lullaby she used to sing to us when Peyton and I were babies. I wish I knew the song, and maybe someday, I'll ask her, but right now just hearing it calms me.

"I messed up."

"It's only school. We can figure it out."

"It's not school."

She pulls away and looks into my eyes. I don't even bother wiping away my tears. "Come on, let's sit. Do you want something to drink?" I shake my head and take a seat on the sofa, which has the most amazing oversized pillows. My mom sits and faces me, reaching for my hand. "What's going on?"

"Do you remember when Noah and Peyton flew in for Ben's birthday?"

She nods.

"And the next day, I came out by myself?"

"I figured Ben was with is family."

I shake my head. "The night of Ben's birthday..." I pause. My throat is tight. It's one thing to finally have a recollection, but to say the words a loud to my mother, is another thing. "I hurt, Ben," I tell her. "And I don't know how to fix things."

She sighs. "I'm not even going to ask what happened because I don't want to invade your privacy. I'm assuming it's a private matter?"

I nod.

"But you want to talk about it?"

I shrug. "I guess what I want to know is, how do I tell someone I want something more from them?"

Mom clears her throat. She starts to smile, which makes me grin in return. "When I met your dad, I wanted nothing to do with him. Your uncle Liam had hired me to be the manager of the band, which was an utter joke. I didn't know anything about the industry, but I had to put food on the table for you girls.

"Harrison was everywhere. It didn't matter where I was or what I was doing, he was there. At first, I thought he was annoying and I wanted him to leave me alone, but after awhile, I started to crave his attention. I'd look to him for validation in the job I was doing.

"Plus, the way he was with you and Peyton... it's hard being a single mom and having this guy bond with your children. I wanted you to always remember your father and was so afraid he would be replaced that I made Harrison feel like crap. I led him on. My emotions were

177

hot and cold. One minute, I wanted to be with him. The next, I wanted him out of our lives."

"And now you can't imagine your life without him?"

My mom shakes her head. "As much as I loved your father, Harrison is my soul mate. I barely knew him, and yet, my heart ached when he wasn't around. For the longest time I thought I was betraying your father and I looked for any excuse to keep Harrison away from us."

"How did everything change?" I ask.

"I found out he was leaving. It was the night of Liam and Josie's wedding. I went to Josie's old house and Harrison was packing. He was going to take Quinn and come back here, and I realized I didn't want either of them to leave. I had already fallen in love with Quinn and the thought of not seeing him every day really hurt me. So I told Harrison he couldn't go."

"And that was it?"

She turns away, looking at the coffee table. If she's trying to hide the smile on her face, she's not doing a very good job. "The rest is–"

"How we ended up a family?"

"Exactly," she says. "You know it took me a while to see the errs of my ways, but in the end it worked out. Are you in love with Ben?"

I shrug. "I don't know. Part of me thinks I am. My heart is broken right now, but the other part questions if it's love or longing because Ben's been my best friend for as long as I can remember. Either way, I've hurt him and he's gone or ignoring me, and I want to fix things. I want to go on a date and see if we're compatible. I don't know,

Mom. I just want Ben back in my life and I don't know how to make it happen.

Again, I find myself in her arms, crying my eyes out. She soothes me, telling me everything will be okay. I want her confidence. I want Ben; in any capacity, he'll take me.

"Be honest with him, Elle. Open your heart and show him that he's welcome. If you put it out there, and he doesn't take what you're offering, that's on him. All you can do is try.

She makes it sound so easy when life is nothing but a complicated mess of emotions. I'll do what she suggests because I have nothing to lose because either Ben and I are something we've yet to define, or we're nothing more than friends.

As long as I have him in my life, I'll be okay.

22

BEN

My phone rings, startling me. The pile of cheap pasta I piled onto my fork falls back into the bowl, splashing the hot chicken flavored sauce everywhere. Okay, it's not a lot, but still. I glance down at my phone and Peyton's smiling face stares back at me. I haven't spoken to her since my birthday, which now that I think about it, is a bit odd. Normally, we've been the once a week type friends who check in with each other. I guess after what happened with Elle, I sort of checked out, which isn't really fair to Peyton.

"Well, hello," I say as I answer the phone.

Peyton giggles. "You're cheery."

"I'm eating. What man isn't happy when he's stuffing food into his mouth?"

"Touché. So what're you up to?" she asks. I can already tell she's fishing, but what I don't know is if it's for Elle or for herself. It could be that Quinn hasn't seen me around and said something to Peyton. I suppose he could say something to Elle, but I'm not sure he would, given he's been upset with her over her partying.

"You're going to be a reporter, and that's what you lead with?"

"Ha! I'm going to be a sideline reporter or sitting at a desk where everything will be typed out for me on the teleprompter. However, if you were one of the players I'm interviewing, I'd lead with: tell me, Ben, you've disappeared. Where have you gone?"

I sigh, pick up my bowl and carry it to the sink. What's left of my lunch is now slipping down the drain, much like my life had been. "I'm in New York."

"Visiting your mom?"

Crap, I forgot to call my mom. I make a mental note to do that when I get off the phone with Peyton if time allows. Glancing quickly at the clock, I don't think I'll have much time, given that my lunch hour is nearly up, but I do need to call her and ask if she'd like to visit. "No, I'm working. I was offered an internship at Omni, and I took it."

"Does Elle know?"

I shake my head, wishing Peyton could at least feel my phone moving back and forth. One of my co-workers walks in, and I say hi, hoping Peyton doesn't mind that I'm ignoring her question. Deep down, I'm hoping she forgets and asks me something else, but I'm only kidding myself thinking she would. The twins remember everything.

"Ben, can you talk right now?"

I look at the clock again and know I can't, but I don't want to have this conversation later either. "Hold on one second," I tell Peyton as I walk back toward my desk. Talia is there and gives me a smile that has so much meaning behind it. We've been growing closer for the past week or so, even though I'm not sure I'm ready to pursue anything with her. I'm tempted, but I don't want to ruin our working relationship. That doesn't mean I haven't thought about her writhing underneath me. Of course, her face always ends up with Elle's by the time my little fantasy plays out.

"Talia, I have to go take this call. I'll be in the conference room if anyone needs me."

She eyes me cautiously. Taking time away from our desks, while allowed, is sort of frowned upon. Our lunches are short because we're expected to be ready for our manager at any given time. I'd probably be the same way if Talia were to say this to me. "Okay, Ben."

I walk away, and when I turn to look over my shoulder, she's staring at me. I'd be an idiot not to pursue something with her. Talia's beautiful, smart, kind and makes me laugh. We're stuck in a work situation and both facing graduation when we return to our normal lives. I don't want to start something we'll both regret later. Yet, I do, because I want to get over Elle, even though I don't imagine I ever will, but using Talia to do it, isn't right and I don't want to hurt her.

I take a deep breath and say, "Okay, I have a bit more privacy."

"Ben, what's going on?"

"It's a long story, Peyton. But, uh... before the quarter ended, I was offered a coveted spot in New York with this firm, and I took it."

"I'm not talking about New York. I'm talking about why you didn't tell Elle?"

The conference room has floor to ceiling windows, much like most of the high rise buildings in New York. From this vantage point, I can see the Statue of Liberty, the greenish woman who greeted millions of immigrants into America, and who represents freedom. Except, I don't feel free because I still feel like Elle is everywhere, trying to invade this tiny bit of solitude I've made for myself, even though it has a looming expiration date. The return to California is going to happen whether I want it to or not, and the lie I've been living will come to a halt.

"Ben?"

"I'm here, Peyton."

"Listen, Elle told me something while we were in Aruba—"

"You went to Aruba?" I ask, interrupting her.

"We did, for spring break. We needed to get away, and we did some wedding planning."

What did Elle need to get away from? Me? Her life? Did she even realize I was gone? "I see," I say as if I'm hurt, and maybe I am even though I have no right to be. I left and told no one. I can't honestly expect the twins and Quinn to include me in everything. Knowing they didn't, really hits home. Coming here was the right thing to do. I need the separation from the Powell-James family, even if it kills me. "What did Elle say?"

"That you guys slept together, and I don't mean taking a nap on her couch, Ben. Did you?"

I close my eyes and images of Elle, throwing her head back as I entered her come rushing back. I've tried to block them out, but it never happens. For as long as I live, I'll be haunted by that night.

"Ben?"

"I'm here."

"Help me understand, Ben, because I don't. I know you love my sister so if you were finally together, why are you hiding in New York?"

"I'm not hiding, Peyton. I didn't tell you or Quinn because I didn't want Elle to know. That night... everything changed."

"But this is what you wanted. I'm confused, Ben."

"Because she didn't remember, Peyton." My teeth clench together. I pinch the bridge of my nose to try to calm down. I'm on the verge of having every emotion come out of me from anger to tears. "She didn't remember," I say again, this time more quietly.

"Oh, Ben," her voice breaks. I'm tempted to hang up now because I don't want to hear the pity in her voice. "Elle remembers. The details are fuzzy, but she knows, and she's been trying to be a better person. She doesn't understand why you lied to her."

"Because I went to kiss her in the morning and she shunned me, asking me what had happened between us. I felt like I had to lie to save face."

Now that I'm on the phone with Peyton, what if I made a mistake by not telling Elle? What if things could've been different if she knew the truth? Or worse. Elle could've easily stopped talking to me, but she didn't. She's tried every day, up until I told her I had a girlfriend, which she accepted and has since kept her distance. Truth is, I miss her and her stupid text messages.

"I'm so sorry, Ben. I know I can't make excuses for my sister and what happened that morning, but I think you really need to talk to her."

"I can't, Peyton. The rejection—"

"I know. I've been there, remember?"

I do, all too clearly. When Peyton finally thought she and Noah were going to be together, a bombed dropped on their little bubble of happiness. It about destroyed Peyton, but also brought us closer. We shared a common theme, being in love with someone who can't or doesn't love you back. I confided in her, things I haven't even told my brother.

"It's too late, Peyton. I took a chance when I knew I shouldn't, and it backfired, in the worst possible way."

"Ben—"

"Listen, I'd appreciate it if you kept my whereabouts to yourself. I don't want Elle to know where I am or what I'm doing. It's best we go our separate ways with graduation coming up and... I just think it's best. Goodbye, Peyton." I hang up before she has a chance to try to change my mind. Exasperated, I pull out one of the executive chairs and sit down, welcoming the expensive leather and well-cushioned padding.

When the door opens, I swing around to find Talia standing there. "Don't get up on my account," she says, laughing. I can't help but smile back, despite the way I'm feeling. Taking the call from Peyton was the last thing I should've done, especially while at work.

"Just testing things out," I say, standing up. Talia steps into the conference room and closes the door behind her.

"I see that. Is everything okay?"

For some reason, I hold up my phone and shake it back and forth, as if it's a clue to what's bothering me. "Just a call from a hometown friend."

"I thought you weren't from one specific place?"

I did tell her and the rest of the team that one night after a round of drinks, mostly because I didn't want people to put two and two together and come up with me having lived in the same town as 4225 West. "We all come from somewhere, right?"

"Yes, we do, but you—"

"I know," I say, hoping she'll stop asking. So far, I've been able to keep my association with the band away from work, even though I had fully intended to use them if need be, at least for advice on my proposal. However, after spending so much time with them over the years and listening to Elle go on about how she's going to be a different manager, I knew what Eo needed in order to get back in the game.

I open the door and motion for Talia to walk ahead of me. My phone vibrates in my hand. I flip it over to see Elle's face and my heart sinks. It's not a coincidence she's calling right after I hung up with her sister, but I'm confident Peyton didn't tell her where I was either. My steps falter as I stare at her picture. I took it the day before Peyton's accident. We had been surfing most of the day, and she decided to go out and do another run. I stayed back and watched, wishing things were different between us. A plan started forming while I watched her surf. I was going to take her out to dinner and open my heart to her. When she came out of the water, the sun was shining perfectly behind her. With a little zoom, I was able to capture her beauty.

The next day, everything changed. While we were in Chicago, I tried to show her I wanted more, but she was closed off and unreceptive. There was a time during the stay at the hospital I thought she was seeing someone. Elle would disappear for hours and come back acting as if she hadn't been gone. I played it off, not wanting to know what she was doing.

The words should've come out of my mouth then. Faced with losing Peyton and all fearing what life was going to be like, I knew what I wanted. I just had to open my mouth and tell her. I think if I had, things would be different right now and my thumb wouldn't be hovering over the Decline button.

23

ELLE

*M*y life has become one of those you see in the movies when a woman is single with no hope of love blossoming soon. Only, I created my situation by not opening my eyes to what was right in front of me, and now he's gone and is taken by another.

I stand at his door, my arm poised to knock. After my session with the therapist, where I relived the night that has been plaguing me for weeks, I came to the realization that I'm a spoiled brat who needs a timeout. I've been treating Ben like he doesn't matter to me when he matters the most, and I shouldn't have come onto him the night of his birthday. But, I did, and now here I am, trying to make amends. I figure I can be the best friend, who is around to hang out and be there to nurse his broken heart when he and Talia break up.

After learning the truth about the night Ben and I were together, my heart broke even more than it has been. My actions were deplorable. The rejection he must've felt couldn't have been easy on him. I can't go back and change the morning after, but I can make things different moving forward.

I've tried calling him, but he refuses to answer. This is a hint that I'm clearly being ignored. If he wants to dissolve our friendship, so be it, but it's not going to happen until I've had a chance to tell him how sorry I am. Not because we slept together, but by the way I acted. He deserves better.

My fist comes down hard on his door, pounding three times in succession. It swings open, the wind causing Talia's hair to blow. She's perfect, and I hate her, and I don't even know her. I smile, it's forced, but it's all I have right now. "Hi, I'm Elle," I say, grabbing her hand. I leave her no choice but to shake mine.

"Hello."

Ugh! Even her voice is soft and sweet. Why can't Ben date someone ugly with warts and finagled teeth? Because Ben's hot. I also came to this conclusion last night as I was lying in bed, trying to remember our night together. My therapist says now that I've unlocked the memories, they'll start flooding back, likely at an importune time. You know, like when I'm in class and suddenly start reminiscing about him going... now is not the time.

"Talia, right? I'm Ben's best friend, and I thought we could hang out."

She turns her head slightly. "My name isn't Talia."

"Oh," I say. "Am I saying your name wrong?" I swear Ben said this was her name. I mean it's been a while since he told me about her, but I'm usually good with names.

"No, well yes. My name's June. Not Talia."

Now I'm the one saying, "Oh." Now, I'm the one who's confused. Why would Ben tell me her name is Talia when it isn't? None of this makes any sense. "Is Ben home?" I try to look over her shoulder, but she moves so I can't see into the apartment. In fact, she's blocking me from entering.

Talia, also known as June, shakes her head rather slowly. The door starts to close, and for the life of me, I can't understand why. "Ben's in New York."

"I'm sorry, what?"

"I thought you said you're his best friend?"

"I am... we had a falling out, and I've been trying to give him space because you're dating."

This time she laughs. "Ben and I aren't dating."

"You're not?"

"No, I'm subletting from him."

As her words sink in, I try not to cry. Ben moved and didn't tell me. Am I that big of a bitch that he'd keep something like this from me. "Oh, right. I'm sorry to bother you." I rush back to the apartment I share with Quinn, slam the door and run to my room where I collapse onto my bed. Tears that have been building for weeks finally come to fruition and pour out of me like a faucet. He left me because I'm selfish, evil, and have made the most deplorable mistake ever.

My door opens, and the smell of Quinn's cologne fills my room. "What the hell is going on?" he asks, sitting down on the edge of my bed. I look at him with my tear-streaked face. His face falls and pulls me into his arms. "Talk to me, Elle."

"I messed up so bad, Quinn. You were right, I need help, but it's too late because Ben's gone."

"What do you mean, Ben's gone?"

"He moved to New York," I say through ragged breaths. "He lied about the girl living in his apartment. He told me her name is Talia and it's not, her name's June, and he's moved. He didn't even say goodbye." I cry louder, and Quinn's grip on me becomes firm. He rocks me back and forth, telling me everything will be okay. But he doesn't know that. No one does. I screwed up and lost the one person outside my family I could count on.

"There's more. I slept with him and acted like I didn't remember." My crying sounds like a wailing child who doesn't get what they want. Typical, Elle.

"Why did you lie to Ben?"

I sit up and wipe away the tears and snot. "I didn't, not at first. I honestly didn't remember. I had so much to drink at his birthday party, and when I woke up, I was confused. My therapist says my mind blocked it out, out of fear of losing Ben, but I lost him anyway because he's gone. What am I going to do, Quinn?"

It's an open-ended question. I know this. His answer could be anything sarcastic, like stop partying, drinking and doing who knows what else. The thing is, I have stopped, and I don't know if Quinn has noticed. However, I stopped too late, and now Ben's left me for good.

"I can't believe he's dropped out of school."

"I know, right? That's so unlike Ben." And it's unlike me to sleep around, but I did that, and now I'm paying the price.

Quinn shakes his head. "I don't know what you're going to do, but wallowing isn't going to help. Get dressed. You're coming with me."

I look down at my clothes and back to him. "I am dressed."

"No, get, like, going out dressed. I have a gig, but I want you to hear the opening act."

My eyes go wide. I'm in no shape or form to go out. Not to mention, he told me he'd never hire me so why would he encourage me to listen to another band. "Quinn..."

He stands and holds my hands. "Listen to me. I know I said some mean stuff, but I've seen changes in you. Big changes and so have Mom and Dad. Come with me tonight and listen to some music. It will take your mind off things. Plus, it might inspire you and remind you of what you want to do."

"The only thing I'm inspired to do is lie in bed and feel sorry for myself."

"Which is code for texting and calling Ben until he answers, right?"

Oh, look, fuzzball. I pick at my comforter, refusing to answer Quinn. I hadn't thought about either of those things because I don't know what I'd say. Calling him earlier wasn't because I wanted to talk... well, it was, but it was to see if he was home, and I wanted to hear his voice because I miss him.

Does Ben miss me? I like to think so, but after learning what I have done, I don't know if I'd miss me if I were him. He's smart to ignore me, move away and do whatever else he's doing.

"What if Ben has a girlfriend in New York?" I ask Quinn out of the blue.

"Random," he says. "And what if he does?"

I shrug.

"Are you saying you like Ben?"

I shrug and feel my cheeks heat up. I shouldn't be embarrassed for liking someone, but it's Ben, and Ben is different. Ben is... well, he's my Ben and always has been. For years, we were accused of dating on the sly, but we never did, and now I'm asking myself why not. What held me back? He has everything I'm looking for if I were looking. Ben's sweet, caring, and family oriented. My parents and siblings love him. His brother doesn't care for me, but whatever. Ben's ambitious and supportive. He's hot, sexy and his smile used to make me weak in the knees. After so many years, I've become immune to his charms, but I don't want to be anymore. I want to be the woman he smiles at and who has to hold onto him so she doesn't trip. I want my best friend back, but I want so much more with him.

"Elle?"

"What?" I say sharply.

Quinn shakes his head but can't hide his smile. "Get dressed, Elle. If you come with me tonight, I'll try to help you out with Ben."

"Really?" I ask, hopping off my bed. "Are you serious, Quinn?"

"Serious, now get ready. I have to leave in ten minutes."

I scream. "Ten minutes!"

"I warned you," he says from down the hallway.

By the time I find something to wear, fix my makeup and put my hair up, it's almost twenty minutes. Thankfully, Quinn didn't leave me behind, not that he would, but he did give me a rash of crap for making him late. I promised to make it up to him later, although I don't know what I'll do.

In the car, I lean over and kiss him on the cheek. "Thank you, Quinn." He pats me on the leg. "I mean it. You've put up with a lot over the years, especially from me and more so lately. You could've ditched out on me, but you didn't."

"And you could've been horrible to me when our parents got together, but you weren't. You and Peyton gave me a family and allowed your mom to become mine. You have no idea how much of an impact having a mom has had on my life."

I pull my brother into a hug and try not to cry. While our dad is amazing, knowing his biological mom didn't want him, has been hard on him, even if he denies it. Our mom though, she stepped up and adopted Quinn.

He finally puts the car in drive and heads toward the club where he's performing. "Do you remember adoption day?" I ask.

"Badoption," he corrects me. We were so young we had no idea what the process was called. All we knew is we wanted our parents to be our parents. "Not so much the actual day, but the day I asked Mom if she'd be my mom forever. I was so nervous, afraid she would say no."

"Peyton and I felt the same way. We were scared that if Dad became our dad, we'd erase our father, but Dad was so adamant that Mason would always be a part of our lives."

"We have great parents, Elle."

"We do, don't we, Quinn."

For a few minutes, we ride in silence. I haven't asked him about the band he wants me to check out, but I'm excited he's thinking about my future. I'd love to sign someone before I finish school. Doing so means I have to start out on my own, and while I know I can do it and have some connections, I think I want to start at the bottom and work my way to the top with a firm, where I can expand my network and really excel. However, there's one more thing I want more.

"I want a love affair like our parents have."

"You mean have three kids and never get married?"

I laugh. He's right. For some reason our parents won't get married, which doesn't matter anymore because they're considered common law, but still. Both have been very adamant a piece of paper won't change anything between them, so why get it. "No," I say. "I want the kind of love where either of us walks into the room, and no one else exists. Noah and Peyton have it. I want it."

"And when you walk into the room, who do you see standing there, waiting for you?"

"Ben," I say. "It's always been Ben. It's just taken me years to figure it all out."

24

BEN

*M*y anxiety levels increase when I step into my cubicle. There's a file on my desk that's the size of a ream of paper, and there's a sticky note from Margie sitting on top of it, asking me to go and see her. From my tiny space, I can see that the light is still off in her office, which gives me time to try and figure out what's going on.

After taking off my jacket, I pull out my chair and sit down, setting my phone next to my monitor. I thought about calling Elle back all through the night, and the temptation was almost too strong to resist. I wanted to know what she wanted, but I couldn't bring myself to make the call. As a result, I was up most of the night, waiting for her usual three a.m. calls. It was sometime between two and four in the morning when I realized I miss those calls. My time in New York is coming to an end, and while I'm not ready to leave because I love this job, I am ready to go back to California to see Elle. Since

I left, her Instagram has been quiet, which is really unlike her. Her last post is a picture of the two of us, taken on my birthday. Seeing it hurts. Not only does it remind me of a night I'd like to forget, but it's reminiscent of a friend I've lost.

"What's that?" Talia asks as she hands me my cup of coffee. This week, she's the coffee runner, filling our orders in the morning. Against my brother's advice, I've splurged on Starbucks because it's what I'm used to. I tried to drink the cheap stuff from the corner bodega, but couldn't stomach it. He'll be surprised to know I haven't spent a penny of his money though, and I plan to give it back to him. I only have to figure out how to do so because Brad won't take it if I hand it over to him.

"I'm not sure. It was here when I walked in." I haven't even flipped the cover yet to see what's inside.

"Looks important. Is it from Margie?"

I nod, agreeing that it does look important. The question is, why's it on my desk and where's Talia's copy? "I think it's meant for someone else." Which it could easily be since my name wasn't on the note.

"You probably won the competition."

"If I did, that means you did as well. They're picking a team, remember?"

Talia sits down in her chair and faces me. "Ashley heard that the managers changed their minds, something about some people outworking their partner."

"Well, they can't be talking about us. We've worked equally as hard." I offer her a smile before turning my attention back to the folder. With my coffee in one hand, I open the file and look at the first page. It's a proposal for a pharmaceutical company. The following pages include their budgets, targets and a copious number of notes by Margie. Still, until she arrives at work, I'm not going to assume anything. Besides, I'm only an intern. For this file to be on my desk, it has to be a mistake.

A mistake that's giving me anxiety as I watch the clock. I've been here for almost two hours, and Margie has yet to walk in. If I could pace, I would, but my other project, the one with Talia, needs my attention. Except as I look at the words, they're blurred. My focus is off and my mind's racing, wondering what's going on.

My cell phone rings. It's Brad. I don't know whether to take it or not so I let him go to voicemail only for him to call right back. This time I answer, "Hello."

"Sup."

"Trying to work," I tell him. Our jobs are so different. If Brad's sidetracked, he can move onto painting or hammering out a dent.

"Job too hard?" He laughs.

"It's challenging. What's up?" I can feel someone staring at me. I look around, expecting to see Margie standing outside her office, but it's Talia, smiling softly. As soon as our eyes meet, she waves. She's cute, and I like spending time with her. Lately, we've gone out with the other interns, and I've thought about asking her out, just the two of us because I'd like to get to know her better. I return the smile but leave the waving to her.

"Just checking in, see what's going on."

"Not much. Work keeps me busy, but I've seen some of the city." Our group has spent Saturdays doing the tourist thing. We've done everything from Rockefeller

Center, Times Square, Coney Island, and have even managed to get tickets to a few baseball games. Nose-bleed seats are cheap unless you're a Yankee's fan.

"Are you ready to come home?" It's like my brother is a mind reader. How did he know this has been weighing heavily on my mind?

"Yes and no. I like it here, and I don't know what I'm coming home to."

"One pissed off hot chick," he says. "You know, I used to think Elle was hot in high school, but as we got older, my thoughts changed on her because I felt she was always leading you on. Now though, she's smoking hot and a complete bitch. I get why you have a hard time staying away from her."

"When did you see Elle?" I ask. It doesn't bother me if Brad thinks Elle's hot. She is. I'm the first one to admit it. I can't even argue with the part about her being a bitch because she can be, even when she isn't trying to be one. As of late, I chalked her attitude up to anger and maybe a bit of depression, but when it boils down to it if Elle doesn't want to do something or isn't getting her way, she lets you know about it.

"She came by, asking where you were."

"When was this?"

"A week or so ago, I don't remember exactly," he tells me. Why did he wait so long to call me? I know better than to ask him, already knowing his answer. It was with his encouragement that I came here and avoided talking to Elle. He's right. I have to forget her and start living my life. Speaking of, I glance to my left to see what Talia's doing. She's typing furiously, likely transcribing our notes from yesterday.

"Oh, right," I say, not wanting to know what Elle wanted with my brother.

"Anyway, I didn't tell her where to find you."

"Thank you." I never thought Brad would tell Elle anything. The last I knew, they couldn't stand each other. "Hey, listen, my boss just walked in, let me call you back later."

"Later, bro." Brad hangs up without giving me a chance to tell him goodbye. He's never been one for the niceties when it comes to a conversation.

As soon as I set my phone down, I pick up the file and head toward Margie's office. Her door is open, but I knock anyway.

"Come in, Ben."

"I won't take long. I believe this is your file. It was on my desk this morning." I hold out the file to her, but she only looks at me.

"Please close the door."

"Um..." I turn and do as she says. When I look back at her, she motions to the chair in front of her desk. The same one I sat in on my first day here.

"There's no question in my mind that you're carrying your team. Talia does fine work, but it's subpar compared to yours. The file I set on your desk is a project I'd like you to work on."

"What about the Eo project?"

Margie shuffles some papers on her desk, pulling out a sheet and handing it to me. Once again, the words blur, but my mind knows exactly what it says. The words 'job offer' and 'position' jump out very clearly. "As you can see, we're offering you a job. This is away from the intern competition going on. You'll be a level II account manager with a secretary and five accounts. It's very rare we offer a job like this to a graduating senior, but your knowledge, work ethic and ability to step in and do work outside of your project has spoken volumes to the senior managers."

"Thank you, Margie."

"No thanks are needed, Ben. You're a rarity, and we'd love to have you on our team. The job would start on July first, giving you time to move and settle after graduation."

I nod and look at the letter again. All the right words are there, making this a dream come true. "Can I think about it?"

"Of course. In the meantime, I want you working on the pharm project. We need fresh eyes on it."

"You got it." I leave her office, but instead of going back to my desk, I take a walk down the hall, wishing I had my phone because I need to call... Elle. She's who I want to call and tell my good news to, but I can't. I won't. Our conversation will have to wait until I'm home and we're face to face.

Back at my desk, Talia watches me as I come down the aisle way. "How about dinner tonight?" I ask.

"Sure, I'll ask the others. What time?"

I shake my head. "Just us." Talia's eyes light up, and she nods. "I'll make the reservation." As soon as I sit down, I glance quickly at Talia, but can only see her shoulders. My guess is she's hunched over, typing on her phone, telling whoever the recipient is of her message that I asked her out. It's a ballsy move, but one I knew she'd say yes to.

The rest of my day goes by seemingly. Even though Talia needs my assistance on our project, I manage to familiarize myself with the pharmaceutical file. Margie and I will meet and go over a plan of action to increase their brand awareness.

Once five o'clock hits, I'm packing up most of my stuff and waiting for Talia. Not once since we started, have we left at closing time. It's probably my fault, and my desire to be the best at everything I do, which seems to have paid off with the job offer. I can't wait to tell Brad, but again, I think it's something I'll do when I'm home. Taking the job seems like a no-brainer, and I'd be stupid to pass it up.

"Where are we going?" Talia asks as she steps out of her cubicle. She places her arm in mine, something she's done from the first day we met.

"I made a reservation at Delmonico's."

Talia stops walking and pulls my arm, making me stop as well. "Ben, Delmonico's is too expensive."

"It's fine, and we deserve a nice treat. Our time is almost up, might as well enjoy it."

"If you say so," Talia says, but there's hesitancy in her voice. She's right when a restaurant doesn't list their menu prices, you know it's way over your budget. But I want to celebrate, even if I can't tell her why. Maybe once the winner of the competition's announced, I'll give Talia my news.

To save a bit of pocket change, we take the subway. It's crowded, more so than usual with everyone being off work at this time and either heading home or going to hit happy hour. After our stop and once we've climbed the stairs to somewhat fresh air, my phone chimes. The number is unknown, which prompts me to look right away. "Shit," I mumble.

"What's wrong?" I show Talia the message from the restaurant, canceling our reservation. "I didn't even know they could do something like that."

"We were on a waitlist but told to arrive either way."

"Huh," she says, not looking impressed. Strike one for Ben. I look around to see what is near. Truthfully, I'm not upset because it's money I don't have to spend, but I did ask Talia out and want to make good on request. "Pizza?" I point across the street to the parlor.

"Perfect."

What should've been a nice long dinner, turns into a quick thirty-minute stop. I'm horrible at the dating game, and maybe that's why I never dared to ask Elle out. Nope, I'm fairly certain I never asked her out because I was afraid she'd say no.

Instead of heading right home, Talia and I decide to walk around town for a bit. It's a nice night, but a bit on the chilly side. That's the one thing I haven't gotten used to, the weather. While it's hot back home, New York is still in their spring stage, and the temperature fluctuates too much for my liking. I miss the warmth of the L.A. sun and honestly can't wait to get back to it.

When we reach our neighborhood, we both stop at the Chinese restaurant and look at each other. "Are you still hungry?" I ask. Talia nods, and we walk in, ordering a few items to take back to our apartments.

"Do you want to come over and watch a movie?" she asks.

"Yeah, that sounds great," I tell her as I reach for her hand. This feels right. Pursuing something with Talia is the right step for me, but doing so means I need to come clean about Elle.

Outside our apartment building, I pull out the key to our security door and hold it open for Talia. She pauses in front of me. "Thank you for tonight."

"I'm not sure why you're thanking me. Nothing has gone as planned."

She shrugs. "Sometimes broken plans make the best dates." Talia stands on her tiptoes and presses her lips to mine. The kiss is warm. Her lips are soft... and everything is wrong because when I close my eyes, I see Elle. In fact, I hear her saying my name, which is ridiculous. When Talia pulls away, I hear my name again. This time I look around, and that's when I see her, standing on the sidewalk, staring back at me.

25

ELLE

Q uinn was right. I needed a night away from myself and going to the club where he was performing was the perfect solution. Not only did I get to see my brother command the stage while watching the women go crazy for him, but I also saw the band Quinn feels needs a chance, and he's right.

The band, four guys with a female lead singer, is very No Doubtesque but more on the Top 40, pop front. They call themselves Unfaithful Perfection. When I asked them what their name meant, none of the members could tell me, making me believe they went to the web and asked the band name generator to create something for them. They're new, and their name can easily be changed.

However, it's what Leah said to me in the course of our conversation when I asked her how the band came together, that struck a chord with me. She told me she was in love with the drummer, Kelvin, and flew across the country to be with him, and that got me thinking, which is why I'm standing outside of Ben's apartment, in the freezing cold, waiting for him to come home.

In a rush, I made Quinn take me back to our apartment, where I completely harassed June for Ben's address. With much reluctance, she handed it over, mumbling something about how annoying I am, all while slamming the door in my face. I booked the first flight out of Los Angeles, and now here I am, waiting.

It's stupid for me to be here. Ben and I haven't spoken in weeks, and when I see him, I'm not exactly sure what I'm going to say. I've thought about smacking him for not telling me about his move to New York, but realize he might take it the wrong way and call the police on me for abuse. I imagine we'll lay eyes on each other and we'll both come to our senses. It'll be like in the movies. We'll run to each other and kiss passionately... until a taxi cab drives by and sprays us with water because that's the type of relationship Ben and I have.

From the time I arrived, I've been tempted to reach out to Ben. In fact, I considered blowing up his phone with random pictures. Not only of the two of us but of the sites in New York, telling him I want to visit those places with him. Peyton and I have been here before, visiting a couple of the local tourist traps, but I've never done it with someone I love.

I do love Ben, but I'm not in love with him, at least not yet. There's something between us, it's been brewing for years, and both of us ignored it. Well I did, because honestly I never knew how he felt. I still don't, but I'm here to find out. Either way, I leave New York with answers.

It's late, and I keep looking at my phone, wondering when Ben's coming home. For all I know this is where he lives, and Talia lives with him. If this is the case, I'll look like a total wench, coming here to beg him to come home. Los Angeles is his home. I'm there and so is his brother, although I have a feeling Brad will move to where Ben is because he always has to play the big brother role.

The people coming and going into Ben's building must think I'm a crazy stalker. Honestly, I'm surprised a police officer hasn't asked me to move along being as I've been sitting on the stoop for hours.

When the sun goes down, I start to give up and head to the corner store for some food. Inside, it's warm and a welcome reprieve from the cold air. I'm not built for winters. I need sun and heat, every day. The only time I like the cold is at Christmas, which needs the snow to make the day magical. Also, skiing, but I have a high-tech snowsuit, and that really keeps the cold out. I should've brought it.

It's when I'm coming out of the store that I spot Ben. I haven't seen him in a while, but can already tell he's lost weight. There's a woman on his arm, which causes me to see red. I know I have no right to be jealous, but I am. He's my Ben, not hers.

The realization that Ben may choose this woman over me hits me like a ton of bricks causing me to gasp for air. What if he's in love with her and tells me to go back to California and forget about him? I'm not sure I can do that. I mean, if he loves her, I'll deal with it.

I stand tall when Ben and his "friend" walk by. He doesn't notice me or even look in my direction. Instead, he's focused on her. What if I'm too late? Although, I probably would've come sooner or begged him to stay had he been honest with me about the night of his birthday.

No, that's not true. It's taken me some time to come to terms with the fact because of me Ben and I are in an uncomfortable and awkward position. But I want the chance to apologize and ask him if he thinks there's anything between us, something solid that we may be able to build a relationship on.

They reach the steps to the apartment, and I call out his name. Of course, with the traffic and people on the street, he can't hear me. He's looking at her, and that's when I see it, the slow motion of her rising onto her toes and him bending down to meet her waiting lips. I cry out, "NO!" but not a single person on the street seems to care.

My feet move faster, all while I keep yelling his name. He pulls away from her and looks around, never seeing me. How can he not see me? My arms wave frantically in the air, and I'm out of breath when our eyes finally meet.

"Ben," I say again, this time breathlessly. His mouth opens. It's as if he's in shock, which he should be. He left me high and dry, so to speak, and now I'm here for his explanation.

"Elle? What're you doing here?"

"Do you know her?" the woman asks. She's not shy about moving closer to him, letting me know they're together. It's fine. Like I said, I just want my friend back. "Wait, you look familiar."

"You don't know her," Ben says. I don't know if he's dismissing her or me with his statement. He takes one step toward me before stopping. Ben looks at his girl-friend and frowns. Yep, I've totally interrupted their night. I should feel bad, but I don't.

"No, I think I do, I just can't place her."

By now, Ben is standing in front of me. I want to reach out and touch his cheek to help soften his furrowed brow. His dark hair is shorter than I'm used to seeing, and I find that I like it a lot. It's his eyes though. They speak volumes. I've hurt him, and I see it in the way he looks at me. I want to wrap my arms around his waist and feel his lips press against my hair, hearing him whisper that everything's going to be okay because when I'm with Ben, my life makes sense.

"What're you doing here?" he asks again, this time his words are soft and meant for me.

"You left me."

He shakes his head. There's torment in his eyes, and I want to take away the pain. "How'd you find me?"

"Well, you see, my neighbor June," I pause on her name, waiting to see if he has anything to say about giving me a fake name. "Became a bit irritated with me when I wouldn't stop asking for your address, so she gave it to me."

"But how'd you know I was here, in New York?"

"June told me after I pounded on your, I mean, her door. Did you think I was going to give up trying to talk to you?"

Ben shrugs. "I sort of hoped you would."

"I think you know me better than that." He nods but

doesn't say anything. He looks over his shoulder, and I lean to the side to find his friend still standing there. "Do you need to go to her, Ben?"

He turns back to me and shakes his head. "I should, Elle. I should tell you to turn around and go back to California, to leave me alone, to let me live a life away from your level of crazy. But you're here, and I can't find the words, even though I just said them."

"Ben?" her voice calls out.

"Give me a minute," he says back to her. "I don't know what to do here, Elle. I never expected you to show up or even care that I've been gone."

His words cause me to step back. "Do you really think I'm that shallow? That I wouldn't care that you moved away and didn't say goodbye? I've been trying to give you space because..."

"Because why?"

"Can we talk inside?" I ask. He nods and turns toward his apartment. I'm praying he doesn't live with her, but if he does, I guess she's going to hear everything. I may have to leave some of the details out, like why I'm truly here though.

"Talia, this is Elle," he says, nodding to me.

"This is Talia?" I ask, watching as Ben's face falls. "I think I'll head to the hotel." I don't give Ben time to say anything before I'm walking down the street. Tears threatened, but I hold them at bay. They need to wait until I'm in the comfort of my suite, where I can cry loudly, and no one will bother me.

"Elle, wait." Ben grabs my arm and spins me around. "Just stop, okay."

"No, I won't. For years we've been best friends and then..." I take a deep breath. "Everything changed. Almost immediately, you disappear and tell me you have a girlfriend named Talia, and when I find you, you're living together." I stop and shake my head, wondering how life became so complicated. *Oh yes, I remember the night well, thanks to my therapist.* "I'm sorry, I bothered you." I turn to leave, but he steps in front of me.

"You don't get to show up here and expect things to be the same as they were in Los Angeles. I'm not the same man I was there. I had to make some changes, and you were one of them, and it kills me, Elle. I hate not having you in my life, but I can't go back there with you, not after—"

"I know."

"What do you mean, you know?"

I square my shoulders and prepare to tell him about the night our lives changed. I didn't want to have this conversation on the street, but I'm left with no choice. "You lied to me, Benjamin Miller. I asked you what happened the night of your birthday and you lied. I knew, deep down, something wasn't right, but I couldn't figure it out. I felt different, and couldn't ask you because you were avoiding me. For weeks, I begged to talk to you, hoping you'd come clean, but you refused. You ignored my calls and texts, and when you finally do get on the phone, you tell me it was a mistake. I know I screwed up, Ben, but you're supposed to be my best friend. You're supposed to call me out on my bullshit. So I'm asking you, what happened the night of your birthday?"

Ben runs his hand through his hair, ruffling the coifed look. "It doesn't matter anymore."

"Are you embarrassed to be with me, Ben?"

"What? Are you joking right now? Any guy would give his right arm to date you, Elle."

"Except you."

He shakes his head. "I've given everything I have to you. I have nothing left." Ben sounds defeated, and I hate it. I hate not hearing the happiness that belongs in his voice.

I grab hold of his collar and pull him down, so we're eye to eye. "The night of your birthday, we slept together, three times to be exact. I remember it all, Ben. Every caress, every kiss and every time you looked into my eyes. I deserve the way you've treated me, but I'm here, asking for your forgiveness and asking you, if maybe, you'd like to go on a date with me and, if maybe, you're willing to let me in and try a relationship because, Ben, I'm a shell of who I should be when you're not around."

"You don't need a man to make you whole, Elle."

"You're right. I just need you." I let go of him and pull out my phone. "I'm texting you my hotel and room number. I'll be there until Sunday night if you want to talk." With that, I leave Ben standing on the sidewalk. I'm tempted to look over my shoulder, but I don't. I want to imagine him standing there, watching me walk away.

26

BEN

When did this become my life? At one end of the street, there's a woman I want to get to know watching me and likely wondering what the heck is going on. At the other end, is the woman I have loved most of my life, putting herself out there for me to take and walking away after pouring her heart out to me. One, I know everything about, while the other; I'm starting to learn. One is safe, while the other is unpredictable and crazy.

I look over at Talia, and she waves. It's her thing. The little finger wave meant to bring a smile to a man's face. It does, and I find myself walking toward her. She reaches for my hand as I climb the stairs. I let her take it even though I'm torn up inside. I have a decision to make, one where someone ends up hurt.

Talia and I walk up the three flights of stairs to our hallway. We stop at her door because that was the plan, to watch a movie and have a second dinner, but I'm not feeling it. "I need to think," I tell her as I pull my keys out of my pocket. I don't bother to make sure Talia gets into her apartment safely before I close my door and press my back into it.

I never wanted Elle to come to New York because I needed this time to put separation between us. I don't know what my plan would be when I went home, but I had thought about spending time with Brad until I could find a new place to live or even now, accept the job offer I have from Omni. Nothing has to change though. Elle can go back home, and I can return to ignoring her. It's been hard, but it was getting easier as the days went by.

Except now that I've seen her my heart's racing like crazy and every part of me wants to go to her, just to be in her presence. Elle's dangerous with how she can bend my will to suit her needs. I'm putty in her hands with the blink of her baby blues. When I should've let her walk away, I chased her down thinking she's mad or hates me, and it's pure torment.

There's a soft knock at my door, but I don't budge. "I set some food out here for you, Ben," Talia says, pushing the knife in my chest even deeper. She's the one I don't deserve. "Ben," she says my name softly. "I remember where I know her from. It's her dad. He's the drummer for one of my favorite bands. I guess it all makes sense now, how you've done so well on our project. She's really beautiful."

I wait for the soft click of her door before I start breathing again. In the years I've been friends with Elle, the band has never been a selling point for me. I love her family as if they were my own, and they treat me the same way. To me, they're the Powell-James family who opened their door to an awkward freshman wanting to hang out with their daughter. By all accounts, Mr. PJ should've booted my ass down the steps the first day I met him. But, he didn't, and I think that's part of my problem. If I lose Elle, I lose the entire family.

However, a family shouldn't be the reason to stay and live with the torture of not having the life I want with the person I want. Friends often go their separate ways. It happens all the time, so why can't Elle and I part?

"Because you're in love with her," I mumble into the open space of my apartment. With that, I search the pockets of my coat for my phone. Sure enough, her name is there, and this time I open the chat window, something I haven't done in weeks, and read her messages up until the time I answered her.

How come I never see you on campus?
Ben, where are you?
I passed last quarter!!
Ben...
Please answer me.
I know, Ben. You can stop hiding now.

I focus on the message where she tells me she knows. It's from a few days ago. She called, and I sent her to voicemail. This must've triggered something in her to start asking June questions. I should've warned June about her, but I honestly thought, especially after I told Elle I had a girlfriend, she wouldn't bother with June. I was wrong. Thinking back to what my brother said, Elle had gone to see him as well, to ask where I was. Maybe leaving without telling her was the wrong thing to do.

Elle thinks I've been hiding. I suppose I have. I couldn't let her see how I felt, knowing she had no recollection of the night we spent together. I didn't want her to see the anguish I was in, how hurt I was that the night we finally end up together, she can't remember a single thing that happened. I guess I was wrong there too, but how do you tell someone you so desperately want to be with, that you slept with and then she shunned you. "Oh, by the way, that thing you do with your tongue..." Definitely a conversation I never planned to have.

I bang my head against the door and close my eyes, hoping that somewhere, somehow, an answer about what I should do comes to me. Unfortunately, all I see is Elle, and right now I can't trust my own judgment.

There's another knock at my door, followed by Talia's voice saying my name. What part of "I need to think" isn't clear? The first time she came over, I get it, she's bringing me food, but why's she here now?

"Ben?" she says right before knocking again. "Your food's getting cold."

Is she staring at my door through her peephole, waiting to see if I've taken the food? I don't want to think the worst of her, but she's starting to annoy me a little. I push away from my door and go into my room to change into jeans and a sweatshirt. I was serious when I said I needed to think. I do. I don't know what I'm doing and whether I should go to Elle or not. These answers aren't written in a manual or notebook for easy reference. Any decision I make will be life changing, and I have to be able to accept that.

With my jacket in hand, I grip the knob of my door, pausing to look through the spyhole to see where Talia is. I can't deal with her right now. Thankfully, she's not in the hallway so as quietly as I can, I open my door, shut and lock it behind me before rushing toward the stairwell.

It's Friday night, the streets of Manhattan are bustling with activities. The bar scene is starting to come alive, the dance clubs are about to open their doors, and for a city that fines drivers for honking their horns, the loud beeping from cars is a bit obnoxious. I walk, with no destination in mind, watching people as they stroll past me. New York, much like Los Angeles, offers a variety of lifestyles here. From young to old, married to single, from straight to gay, this city has something for you.

I find myself in the middle of Times Square, climbing the giant red steps until I've reached the top. From here, I can see everything and everyone. In front of me, a man has his arm around his girlfriend, and he's whispering into her ear. I'm curious about their relationship, wondering how long they've been together and if she's the one for him. If she is, how'd he know? All along, I've thought of Elle as being the one for me, but lately, I've been questioning why she is, given that we've never even been together. How can I be in love with someone who I've never dated? Is it even possible?

The people watching soon grows boring, and I'm back on the street, walking away from the tourists who gather to watch the mega billboards and the odd people who dress up as characters. There's a man who dresses up as a baby, complete with a diaper. It's creepy, and in my opinion, he should be arrested. For what, I don't know.

Up ahead, the marquee from the Manhattan shines brightly in my direction. Even without knowing it, I've walked to her hotel. I stop at the front door, and the bellhop opens it for me, but I hesitate. What happens when I go in? I haven't a clue, I just know I need to see her.

Her floor is quiet, not that I expected a place like this to have a ruckus party, but you never know. I knock on her door and wait longer than I expected. When she finally opens the door, she stands there in one of her stupid little tank tops and boxer shorts on. As soon as I step in, she lets the door slam shut behind me.

Now, what do I do? Part of me wants to sit on her couch and talk things out, while the other half of me wants to kiss her senseless. I have no idea what part will win out, that is, until she steps in front of me and removes my jacket, tossing it onto the floor. My hand finds the sweet spot on her hip, touching her exposed skin to my cold flesh.

"I'm sorry my hand's cold."

"It's okay, Ben."

I've always loved the way my name sounds coming from her lips. "Did you mean what you said earlier about going on a date?"

When Elle looks at me, her lower lip is between her teeth. I cup her face and let my thumb pull her lip down. Its plumpness is tempting me to place my mouth on hers.

"I meant every word. It's taken me a long time to realize that each time I look for love, that each time I look at my parents or my sister and Noah, wishing I had what they have, that the person who could give me unconditional love, has been in front of me for years. I've just been too blind to see that it's you." She takes my hand and leads us over to the sofa. When we sit, our thighs are pressing together. I shouldn't get excited as this is nothing new for us. We've always been this close.

"I will never forgive myself for the way I treated you the morning after your party. I was a cold-hearted bitch, and I wish I could tell you why I blocked it out, but I can't. All I know is that I remember the night fully, Ben, and it was amazing. I've never felt so connected to someone, except for you. I don't deserve you. You and I both know it, but I'm asking for a chance. We may not be right for one another, but we'll never know if we don't try."

"What about the partying, Elle? The drinking?"

"I haven't touched alcohol since your party. I knew something was different when I woke up, but when you told me nothing had happened, I don't know... it was like a wake-up call."

"And the other guys?"

She shakes her head. "There's no one else, Ben." Her fingers brush through my hair as if it's the most natural thing to do. Looking at her, it's hard to believe I've been with her, but my body has no qualms about wanting her.

With my hands on her hips, I pull her onto my lap until she straddles me. "Am I making a mistake here?"

"No, I don't think you are. It took you leaving for it all to hit home. You're not just my best friend, Benjamin.

You're the only person I look forward to seeing every day. Your voice is my coffee, my kick-start to start my morning off right. For weeks on end, I've wandered around campus, looking for you, needing just to see you so I could feel right again."

How is it we can both feel the same way and never tell each other? None of this makes sense, and instead of overthinking it and beating the "what ifs" to death, I lean forward and brush my lips against hers, testing her responsiveness. Elle reciprocates fully, wrapping her arms around me and plunging her tongue deep into my mouth, all reminiscent of the night that changed us forever.

27

ELLE

*A*ny reservations I had about Ben are gone. His hands and lips feel perfect against my body. The sensations I'm feeling are like no other. I'm anxious, and I have butterflies in my tummy. I'm nervous because I'm afraid he's going to pull away.

That he might realize this isn't what he wants, Yet, I'm so over the moon happy because he's here and in my arms, and he's kissing me.

Ben and I part, and I use this opportunity to rub my thumb over his freshly kissed lips. I can't help the smile that spreads across my face. Everything about this moment feels right and perfect. That is until Talia's face pops into my mind. I disengage from Ben, despite his attempt to hold onto me.

"What's wrong," he asks.

"Talia. Isn't she your girlfriend? Because you said she was and we were just kissing... I don't want to come between the two of you." There's a pinch in my heart, thinking Ben is already committed. It'd be my own fault for waiting so long, for not asking him again when he started pulling away what really happened the night of his birthday. This would be karma at its best, and I deserve it.

"If she were my girlfriend, I wouldn't have kissed you like I just did and I definitely wouldn't be here, sitting on your couch, thinking about how much I want to be with you right now."

"I'm a bit confused. Do you live with her?"

He shakes his head. "No, we work together. We're part of an internship at Omni."

"Omni? Oh, Ben, that's wonderful." I'm truly happy for him. Omni is the best marketing company in the world according to my dad.

"It's a dream come true."

His words give me pause. His hopes and dreams, they should be my priority as mine has been his. He came with me to California because I asked him to, even though I knew he would excel at a different school. But, the thought of being away from him for years, and only seeing him on vacations made me physically ill.

What kind of friend am I? I get up from the couch and pace the small living area of my suite. I'm tense, and my hands fidget with anything they can touch. I tug at the hem of my shirt. My hands push into my hair, pulling it from side to side. I bite the end of my nail and pick at the skin around it until I dig too deep, causing me to cry out.

Ben's hands are on my shoulders. He's comforting me when I don't warrant his affection. "I'm such a horrible person," I say, turning to face him. "You... you've been my rock for years, and I've been nothing in return. I should've never asked you to move to Los Angeles. How can you stand me?"

"Because I love you," he says as if it's the simplest answer ever.

"But why, Ben?"

He gently holds his hands against my cheeks and looks into my eyes. "You make me smile, Elle. I laugh when I'm with you, and when we're not together, my heart doesn't feel the same. I can't tell you why or how, but to quote Selena Gomez, the heart wants what it wants, and my heart wants you."

"Your heart is familiar with me."

Ben pushes my hair behind my ear, never breaking eye contact with me. "From the moment I met you, I fell hard. I chased Peyton in the hallway because I was adamant she was you, and when I saw you sitting at the table, it was like the sun was only shining down on you. You gave me the time of day when you could've easily told the new kid to get lost."

"I thought you were hot."

"And we became friends because that's what my mom told me to do. She said friends first, but Elle, every time we went out, I wanted to kiss you goodnight. Every vacation we went on, I told myself this would be the moment, and yet I never said or did anything."

"Why not?" I step a bit closer and place my hands on his waist. Ben smiles and pulls me to him.

"I was afraid of ruining our relationship. At that time, I'd rather have you as my best friend than anything else."

"What changed?"

Ben leans down and kisses the tip of my nose. I want more, but not until he answers the question about Talia. "Peyton's accident really hit home. When I saw her in the hospital, I had this moment. I realized I didn't want to be your best friend anymore. I wanted more. I wanted us to build a life together, start a family."

"You wanted, but not anymore."

"Bad choice of a word," he says. "I still want it, but up until you accosted me on the street, I had no idea how you felt."

I step out of his grasp and turn toward the sliding glass door. The city is still alive and bustling with activity. The last time I was here, I rarely left the hotel room or the tour bus. Most of the time when my sister and I, and sometimes Ben, would tour with the band, we were isolated, or we didn't have time to explore. It all depended on schedules.

"Up until the night of your birthday, I hadn't looked at you as anything more than a friend." I stare out the window with Ben's reflection behind me. "There was a girl, she was flirting with you, and I saw red. I thought, 'what is she doing with my man?' and I had no right to interfere, but I did. I was drunk and acting stupid, and yet you placated me when you should've told me to go home. We fought, I remember that clearly." I turn to face him. "What I blocked out was when we started kissing and how I started taking your clothes off. You asked me if I were sure and I said I was. I wanted to be with you Ben, please never doubt that."

"Then how do you explain the morning after?" he asks.

"Fear. Being afraid I ruined the best thing in my life." I shrug. "My therapist says I blocked it out because I was scared that our friendship was over."

"Therapist?"

I nod. "I've been going. She helped me remember that night, and once I did... God, Ben I'm so sorry. I shouldn't have acted the way I did. You deserve so much better than me."

Ben rushes toward me, his mouth colliding with mine. It'd be so easy to get lost in this kiss, to tangle our limbs together between the sheets and forget everything, but I can't. I find myself pulling away again.

"Elle," he whispers my name with so much passion, my knees buckle. What I wouldn't give to be able to love him freely right now.

"Tell me about Talia. I know you, Ben. You must feel something for her."

Ben takes my hand and leads me over to the sofa where we sit down together, our thighs touching. "Like I said, we work together. We live across the hall from each other because that's where our manager put us. I guess for weeks we've sort of been dancing around each other. I've been hesitant because I'm in love with you, the quarter is almost over, and I just wasn't sure."

"But you like her, unless you go around kissing people for the fun of it."

Ben smiles. "No, I do like her, but she's not you, and honestly, that's been my biggest battle, trying to get over you."

"When were you under me?"

Ben laughs and shakes his head. "Seriously? You're going to quote Ross right now?"

I shrug. "We are in the city. I figured why not."

Again, Ben starts playing with my hair. His jovial expression turns serious. "I've been under you, your spell, or whatever it's called, since freshman year. And honestly, I'm glad I have, but moving forward, I'd love the chance to put you under mine, to show you what kind of man I am."

Kiss him, you crazy fool. "And Talia?"

"I need to talk to her. I owe her at least that, plus an apology. She's really sweet and kind, and honestly, if I weren't in love with you, I'd pursue something with her."

"You told me she was your girlfriend. You led me to believe you were living with her."

Ben pulls back and sighs. "I'm not happy about lying to you, but I didn't know any other way. I thought if I told you I had a girlfriend, you'd leave me alone. What I didn't count on was you realizing I was gone. Stupid, on my part, but thought you wouldn't notice, especially since I started separating myself from you."

"Because I didn't remember?"

He nods.

I grab his cheeks and turn him to face me. "Why didn't you tell me? Why not yell and scream at me? Confront me? I knew something had happened, but I couldn't figure it out. When Peyton and I went to Aruba, Noah had made sure the plane had roses and champagne for her, and I told her I wanted a love like hers. She told me I had it if I opened my eyes and finally looked at you.

I told her then that I thought we slept together but wasn't sure. All week, I thought about you and what you were doing, wondering if you missed me half as much as I missed you."

"Believe me, I have."

"So why not tell me, Ben?"

He inhales deeply and looks away. Ben pushes his thumb and index finger into his eyes. He does this when he's about to cry. "I was afraid you'd tell me it was a mistake and I'd rather live with you not remembering than hating me for the rest of my life."

"Oh, Ben," I cry out as tears start to fall from my eyes. I climb into his lap and pepper him with kisses, ones I hope he wants from me. "I could never hate you, even when you were trying to push me away. I've spent count-less hours trying to figure out my life, and the only thing that makes sense to me is you. You've been my constant for as long as I can remember and I don't want to give that up unless you do."

Ben's arms wrap around my waist. "Not a chance in hell. I've been waiting for you for a lifetime."

"Can we try, Ben? Can we date and see if our connection is real, and not based on years of friendship? I want us to be sure, the both of us."

"I'll happily date you, Elle Powell-James. Starting with tomorrow morning. Can I show you the city?"

I nod. "I'd really like that, but first we need some sleep." I slip off his lap and take him by the hand, pulling him into the bedroom. The comforter's pulled back from when I was lying in here earlier. I kneel on the bed and look at Ben. "What's wrong?"

"Nothing, except if I stay here, I'm going to want to touch you and I think we should wait."

"Wait for what?" I question.

"Until we're sure. Sex complicates things."

"We've slept in the same bed before, Ben. We can put a pillow between us."

Ben laughs as he comes into the room farther. He takes my hand and kisses the top of it. "I'm in love with you, and I'm not asking you to say it back to me, I am asking that you let us take things slow, let our relationship build until the point where we know without a doubt that we want to be together."

"I can do that," I tell him. I rise on my toes and place a kiss on his lips. "Until tomorrow."

"Bright and early. I'll pick you up." Ben kisses me again. It's short and perfect and leaves me longing for more. "Sweet dreams, Elle."

28

BEN

*I*t seems as if the only thing I'm really good at right now is leaving Elle. Evident by the fact that I'm walking alone back to my apartment and she's blocks away, after asking me to stay. The decision I made was the right one though. Had I stayed... well, I don't think having a pillow between us would've kept me away from her. What started tonight, is what I've been waiting for - a chance. A chance to finally prove my worth to her, to show her I can be everything she wants in a man and more.

The walk back to my place takes no time at all, and before I know it, I'm looking up at Talia's window. Her light is on, which means she's likely awake and reading or hopefully working on our project. Even though I have the job offer, I still want to win the competition.

I take the steps two at a time, hurrying until my closed fist is poised to knock on her door. I feel like I've done something wrong by kissing Elle tonight, and in hindsight, I suppose I had considered kissing Talia on a few occasions before we were interrupted. I don't expect Talia to understand or forgive me, but I'm going to apologize to her and pray she doesn't slap me in the face, although, I deserve an ass beating.

After a few minutes of silence, the locks start to disengage. She opens her door but leaves the chain attached, preventing me or anyone else for that matter, from stepping into her apartment.

"Can we talk?"

"It's late," she says.

"I know. I'm sorry, but I want to explain what happened tonight." Talia closes the door, removes the chain, and reopens it quickly. She steps aside and allows me to walk into her studio. Her apartment is different from mine. Whereas my walls are bare, she's put up tapestry and placed scarves over lamp shades to give her a place a homey feel. I guess I didn't care that much or didn't want to get attached. I can easily say I won't live in this block when I come back for the job, that's if I take it.

"Do you want something to drink or eat? We have all that Chinese food left." My stomach does a little flip and starts to gurgle at the thought of food. I'm hungry, but I don't feel right eating here. I'm not sure Elle would understand, and if there's one thing I've learned, I can't keep secrets from her.

"I'm good but thank you. Mind if I sit down?"

Talia nods. I take the chair, leaving the couch for her. I don't want to give out the wrong impression by sitting on the sofa. When she comes into the room, I try to smile, but it feels forced, so I stop. "So... how do you know Elle?"

"I'm sort of curious how you know her, honestly."

"I'm a huge fan of 4225 West. I've followed them forever. I don't know why I didn't pick up on it sooner, but I've seen your pictures. You're sometimes with the band. As soon as I figured out who she was, I went and double-checked, and sure enough, there you are, with Elle."

I've heard of fans knowing everything about the band, but have never encountered one. What are the odds? "We've been best friends since our freshman year in high school."

"Best friends, huh? You looked a little closer than BFF status."

"Yeah, that's what I want to explain. You see, before I came here, Elle and I..." I pause and clear my throat. "Things changed between us and neither of us took the change very well. We both made rash decisions and hurt each other in the process."

"I see," Talia says. She pulls her legs up underneath her and spreads a blanket over her lap.

"This is pretty hard for me because I'm not this type of guy. The thing is, I like you, Talia or I wouldn't have kissed you, but I'm in love with Elle, and it wouldn't be fair to you if I were always thinking about her."

Talia looks away. Her fingers play with the frayed end of her sofa. "I wish you had told me from the beginning."

"I didn't know how Elle felt, and honestly I was trying to get over her and move on."

"But she showed up here?"

"I didn't know she was coming, Talia. If I had—"

"You wouldn't have kissed me," she states.

I nod. The kiss was nothing more than a peck but had the potential to be more. Although, I don't know how far I would've taken things with her. She's still my co-worker, and the last thing I want is to be involved with someone from work.

"Well, I guess I can't compete with Elle James, I mean just look at her." Elle is beautiful, but it's not right for Talia to put herself down like this.

"Talia, you're a beautiful woman. Please don't put yourself down. My life before I came here was complicated and it probably still is. Elle and I have this history and-"

"Well, thanks for telling me. I appreciate it." Talia interrupts me. She stands and goes to the door, and opens it, giving me my cue to leave.

"I'll see you Monday?"

"Sure," she says, shutting the door instantly. I stand in the hall, making sure Talia locks the door before I retreat into my apartment. It's cold and lonely inside these walls, and I'm tempted to go back to Elle, but I don't want to cross the line again until we're both sure we can make this work.

❧

I'm up well before I know Elle will be awake, but I can't wait any longer. I'm not even bothered by my lack of sleep or the fact that I'm starving. On my way to Elle's hotel, I stop at one of the vendor carts and pick her up a bagel. In my opinion, you haven't lived until you've spent a considerable amount of time eating street food and New York City has some of the best.

I knock on her door while simultaneously taking a bite of breakfast burrito. It takes her a minute or two, but when she finally opens it, I smile. Not because Elle is standing in front of me, but because it's the Elle I've missed so much. The one who isn't put together, whose hair is in complete disarray, whose eyes are barely open and has makeup smudges on her face. This is my Elle, the one no one, aside from her family, ever gets to see. I lean through the door and kiss her quickly before stepping inside.

"It's so early."

"I know, but we have a busy day. I figured we only have today, right?"

"Yeah." She yawns. "I have class on Monday, so I'm flying back tomorrow."

I hand her the tin foiled wrapped bagel. "What's this?" she asks.

"Breakfast."

"I could've called us room service." She takes the package from my hand and slowly opens it. I follow her to the couch and sit next to her, waiting for her to take a bite. "Oh, this is good."

I can't help but smile at her reaction. "I'm glad you like it."

"Where'd you get it?"

"The street vendor," I tell her.

She closes her eyes. "I love food truck food. It's the

best." Elle knows I'm not going to argue with her. This one time, we went to Malibu to go surfing and drove all over, looking for the right taco truck. Once we found it, we gorged ourselves until well past sundown.

"Do you remember that time in Malibu?"

I lean over and kiss her cheek. "I was just thinking about that trip. We should go back this sum..." I let my words trail off.

"What is it?"

"I was offered a job here, at Omni, after graduation."

Elle looks up and smiles. "You should take it."

"What?"

"Seriously, take it. You deserve it, Ben. I know how hard you've worked."

"Yeah, but—"

"No buts." Elle turns to face me and reaches for my hand. A sense of dread washes over me. I knew last night was too good to be true. She's going to tell me she's changed her mind and that we'll never work. "The night before I flew out here, Quinn took me to see this band he likes, and I like them. As soon as I graduate, I'm going to sign them, along with Quinn. I thought long and hard about what to do. My options are to start at the bottom somewhere or go out on my own. I like the idea of being out on my own, however, if I come to an agency with a strong core of talent under me, I think I have a better chance at being taken seriously."

"That's great, Elle. But what does this have to do with me living here?"

"Don't you see?" she says, cupping my face. "There's so much untapped talent here. I can be here with you, working and discovering the hidden gems. I'll have to travel, but New York can be my home."

"What about your parents?"

She looks at me oddly. "What about them?"

"I don't know, I just thought..."

"Peyton and Noah aren't going to live in California. She wants to work for ESPN, and I think they're out of Connecticut or someplace over here. Besides..." Elle reaches for my hand and threads our fingers together. "It doesn't matter where we live, as long as we're together."

I couldn't agree more, but graduation is approaching, and I don't know if we'll be at the stage of living together by the time I start my job here, although knowing Elle's in the city and not living next to me won't sit very well. I've grown far too accustomed to having her within a few feet of me.

"And you want to live with me?"

"Ben, I meant what I said last night. I want to try. I'm jumping with both feet into a Ben and Elle relationship, complete with cheesy selfies on my Instagram, Facebook relationship status change and ridiculous text messages throughout the day telling you how much I miss you and can't wait for you to come back to California."

I roll my eyes, but the grin I have on my face tells her I'm only kidding with her. "I should run for the hills. You already seem clingy."

"I am clingy, and you should totally run. I have so much to make up for. It's not even funny. What I've done to you, I'll never forgive myself."

"I like your kind of clingy." Without pause, I pull her to me and kiss her lips. Elle responds immediately, pushing me back into the sofa. For a swanky hotel, this couch is incredibly uncomfortable, but the girl I love is laid out on top of me, making me not care about a potential backache.

Elle and I make out like two horny high school kids whose parents aren't home. This is what I've wanted, to be in her presence this way, to know her intimately and be the man she calls hers.

When we part, her lips are red and swollen, and her hair is even more messed up than before. "You're so beautiful," I tell her. "How'd I get so lucky?"

"You sat down and saw the real me, not the one our classmates saw, the who has a famous family. The fame, it never mattered to you, and I was always just your Elle, your best friend. It's not a case of how you got lucky, but more so of how I got so lucky. You're the best thing to ever happen to me, Benjamin. There isn't a day that goes by that I don't remember the first day we met."

"Me neither," I tell her and promptly go back to kissing her.

29

ELLE

here's nothing like kissing Ben. And to think I would've never fully experienced the act if my sister hadn't opened my closed-off mind to the possibility of Ben being the one for me. I wish I could go back, months or even years, and stand outside of the relationship Ben and I have, and really take a look at what we were doing. So much wasted time has gone by. No, it wasn't lost in a sense we weren't together, but we could've been so much more.

Kissing your best friend is not awkward, at all. I thought it would be, which is probably the most significant part of my hesitation in believing Ben could be the one for me. Yet, I can't imagine anyone else making me feel the way I do. The warm and fuzzy sensation coursing through my body is everything a first love is supposed to be. It just sucks that we've waited so long. Well, mostly me. I have no doubt Ben would've jumped at the opportunity if it had presented itself much earlier.

However, we're here now, and we're going to try, and I'm going to do my damnedest to make things work, which is why I told him I'd come with him to New York. Without a doubt, I'll move anywhere he's going to be because building a relationship thousands of miles away from each other isn't the right way to start off. I told him, both feet in, and I mean it. There's no going back, only moving forward.

"I'm going to take a quick shower," I tell him, except his arms tighten around my waist, pinning me to his body. "Bennnn..." I draw out his name in exaggeration.

"Stay," he says. His voice is raspy, sexy. I want to stay, but Ben's right, sex complicates things, and as much as I'd love to stay locked up in this hotel room, being outside with him and touring the city where we're going to live is important to me.

"You promised me a date," I remind him, looking deep into his eyes. "And cheesy pictures to decorate my social media with." I wink, but he knows it's true.

Ben groans and closes his eyes. He's the one who knocked on my door at seven a.m. with breakfast. Mind you. It's one of the best bagels I've ever had. I would've never thought a grilled bagel could be so delicious.

I finally peel myself away from Ben. Our combined body warmth dissipates too quickly for my liking. Inside the bathroom, I take a look at myself. My lips are swollen, and there's a slight rash forming from Ben's whiskers. My finger brushes along my mouth as a smile breaks out until my eyes land on my hair. "My God, Elle, next time look in the mirror before you answer the door for your boyfriend."

Boyfriend.

I love the sound of calling Ben, my boyfriend.

What's even better, is Ben doesn't care what I look like in the morning. He's seen me at best, and certainly at my worst. There are no secrets between us.

I take a quick shower, just as I promised Ben I would. When I step out of the bathroom, he's hunched over, alternating between writing on a pad of hotel issued paper and searching on his phone.

"What're you doing?" I ask, keeping my distance from him. I'm naked under my robe, and the last thing I want to do is to start touching him. I won't stop because I'm eager to be with him again and be fully aware of everything going on between us.

"Mapping out our day."

I roll my eyes. Ben's a planner, always has been. It's not a bad thing, but sometimes you have to just go with the flow. "Don't want to be spontaneous?"

Ben sets his pen down and looks at me. His eyes travel down the front of the fluffy white robe I'm wearing before turning back toward the paper. He clears his throat. "I thought if you're going to move here, we'd hit the neighborhoods and decide where we're going to live."

"I heard Tribeca is a nice place."

Ben shakes his head. He stands and comes to me. I expect him to keep a sizable distance between us, but he doesn't. His fingers start to play with the wet strands of my hair, while his other hand rests on my hip. "It's expensive there and out of my price range. My starting salary is nice, but I don't want to struggle. I want us to have a life and do things."

"Ben—"

He holds his hand up, cutting me off. I have a feeling he knew what I was about to say. "Can we try to make it on our own? If we have a place that I can afford, anything you earn from your business will be butter. I know you can easily buy any home you want, but I'd really like the opportunity to take care of you."

"But you don't have to. You know that, right?"

"I know, Elle. I know you have a trust fund and two parents who will do anything for you, but this is a pride thing for me."

I nod, conceding an early defeat. I'm not going to argue with Ben because this seems important to him. "So what areas are we visiting today?"

Ben's serious expression turns to one of elation. "I thought we'd visit Nolita, Murray Hill, and Brooklyn Heights, mostly because I know how much you love the townhouses."

"With those massive wrought iron railings?"

Ben nods, and I clasp my hands together. "I'm going to get dressed and do my girly stuff. I'll rush so we can go." I go to step around Ben, but he traps me. When I look at him, the happiness he was showing a few seconds ago, seems to be gone. "Ben?"

"Are we really doing this, Elle? Looking for a place for us, as a couple?"

"It only makes sense, at least to me. We've known each other for eight years, Ben. We've seen each other at our best, and worst. I think if we're living apart from each other, we'll end up together, wasting money on a place neither of us will use."

"Okay," he says, but he looks reserved.

My hand cups his face, and I use what little strength I have to pull him down for a kiss. When we part, I can't keep the smile off my face. I feel sorry for Quinn right now because I'm on cloud nine with the amount of happiness I feel. "Unless you tell me we're not."

"I'll never," Ben whispers. "Being with you, it means everything. I don't want to spend a single minute away from you."

"Then I guess you have your answer." This time Ben does let me go so I can get ready for our day. As promised, I work quickly to get prepared, opting for a lighter look with my makeup. Thankfully, I brought along a beanie along with me so doing my hair, other than blow-drying, isn't needed.

In the main room, I find Ben relaxed, watching the news. I stand there for a second before he turns his gaze to me. "Ready?"

"I am," he says, turning off the television. "We're going to cram as much as we can into today," he tells me as he opens the door. "And eat so much food."

"Let me guess, New York has an app to locate food trucks?"

Ben chuckles. "Actually, I don't know. I'm not sure one is needed since every corner has a vendor on it."

The air is brisk, but the sun is shining. I'm going to have to get used to the colder temperatures and the snow, which doesn't make me happy, but I'll survive. Ben and I will have to take a lot of mini vacations south of the equator or at least fly home to see my parents.

Ben takes us to the subway and tells me to be careful

as we descend the steep stairs. The tunnel reeks, and I try not to let it bother me. I don't know if public transportation will be my thing or not. It's not something I've ever had to use. Growing up, my parents, grandfather or any one of my aunts and uncles, would drive us everywhere until we were old enough to drive ourselves. My siblings and I are spoiled, and our needs are catered for.

"Is this how you get to work?"

"Yeah."

"What are you going to do with your car?"

Ben sighs. "Probably leave it with Brad for a bit, while I make sure this is where I want to be. If we decide to stay, I'll sell it."

I lean into Ben and hold onto his arm while we wait for the train. He tried showing me the map of the system and explaining things, but it looks so complicated. Too many trains to choose from, and different lines, not to mention if you take the wrong exit, you end up on the wrong side of where you want to be.

Once we're on the train, I sit down while Ben stands next to me. It's crowded, and everyone is forced to violate the personal space issue. Ben doesn't take his eyes off of me though, and I have a feeling he's watching and waiting for a temper tantrum.

"I'm fine," I tell him, even though I don't believe my own words. This will take some adjustments, but it'll work out.

Ben grips my hand tightly when it's time for us to get off. I breathe a sigh of relief when we're back above ground. He leads me across streets, and by others, in a rush to get to our destination.

"A park?"

"Not just any park," he says, weaving in and out of trees until we come to a wall, keeping the bay away from us. "Look," he says, pointing out toward the harbor.

"Wow, she looks so small." Out in the middle of the water is the Statue of Liberty. "I've only seen her from the plane."

"You need a reservation to actually take the tour, which usually has to be booked three to six months in advance."

"So, no spur of the moment arrivals from your best friend."

Ben looks down at me. "Girlfriend."

I smile and nod. "I like that." After we take a selfie with just a small bit of the statue in the background, Ben takes me to every possible spot he can, including the neighborhoods he thinks we'll like to live. Of course, I fall in love with Brooklyn Heights, and he promises we'll come back after graduation to really look at places to live.

We stop and eat pizza in Little Italy, like tourists. The thought makes me giggle, but I love it. When we visit Times Square, we take another picture together, and I post this one. The caption is a heart, and my sister is the first one to respond with, "It's about time."

"Peyton agrees." I show Ben while we're sitting on the steps, people watching. He puts his arm around me and kisses my cheek.

"It's because she knows how I feel about you."

I look at him oddly. He doesn't shy away. "Explain."

"When she was in the hospital we bonded over being in love with people who didn't love us back. She encouraged me to tell you, but I couldn't. For the longest time, I thought you had a boyfriend."

"Why would you think that?"

The people in front of us leave, and Ben uses the space to stretch his long legs. "You kept disappearing from the hospital. You'd be gone for hours."

"Why didn't you just ask me where I was?"

Ben shrugs. "I didn't want to hear that you were with someone. I liked the bubble I was in, I guess."

"Ben?"

He turns his head to look at me.

"I was at the church across from the hospital, praying. Asking whoever would listen to save my sister, to not put my mom through the same thing she went through with my father. To ask that my dad and brother be spared from losing someone they love so much. While I was there, I met the priest, and I kept going back because he gave me hope when I was so ready to give up on her. When Noah first arrived, I told him to say goodbye to Peyton because I was so sure she was going to die. Without even trying, I had already expected the worst, and I hated myself. When she woke, I needed someone to tell me that I'm not a horrible person."

"And did they?" he asks.

I shake my head. "Not until the morning after your birthday. I sat on the beach, wondering how my life became such a mess, and all I did was think about you. If it wasn't for that night, I don't know if I'd be here right now."

Ben presses his lips against mine, keeping things

brief. "Well, thank you for shunning me. It's been the best birthday yet." He smiles, and while I know he's joking and trying to make light of the situation, I can't help but feel like I almost destroyed everything important to me.

30

BEN

*S*ince Elle returned to California, I've submerged myself in my work. Not only on the joint project Talia and I are working on but also the pharmaceutical one as well, familiarizing myself with everything. After telling Elle about it, she suggested I take a step back from doing any work on it until I've accepted the job and my contract was signed. She feared Omni was taking advantage of me and wanted me to protect myself. I heeded her advice and informed Margie, who surprisingly agreed.

Now all there was left to do, was sign my contract. Each time I pulled it out to add my signature, I stopped. Working for Omni is my dream, so I don't understand why I'm hesitating to accept employment. It could have something to do with Elle, but I'm not sure what. She's already agreed to move here, and she's right, she can do her job from anywhere. In the two weeks since we've last seen each other, things have returned to normal. Well, as normal as Elle and I can be living three thousand miles apart from each other. The time difference flat out sucks. By the time she's finished any homework, I'm already in bed. When I'm up and walking to work, I text her, even though I know she's still sleeping. All I know is that in a few days, Elle and I will be together again.

When I took her to the airport, we had a proper good-bye. Something we should've had when I flew out to New York, but the both of us were battling some inner demons. Mostly, stubbornness. I should've told her when she asked about our fateful night, instead of lying to her, and she should've demanded answers from me. I suppose it was easier for us to pretend everything was okay when it wasn't. Lesson learned by both of us.

I smile at Talia as I approach my desk. Thankfully, things between us have been good, except she asks a lot of questions about 4225 West, which makes me uncomfortable. I get that she's a fan, but some things are better left unknown, like what kind of underwear Liam wears and if Harrison and Katelyn have an open relationship because they're not married. The latter question bothered me the most because they're my family. When I told Elle, she said it was common and suggested I stay away from looking at the comments people post on the band's Instagram. Again, I took her advice and promised not to look.

"Today's the big day," she says, handing me a cup of coffee.

"Thank you," I say as I set it down on my desk, along with my bag. "Are you nervous?" Even though I have a job lined up, if I decide to take it, I'm still nervous. There's a certain amount of pride that comes with winning a competition, and honestly, I want to win. I want this for both Talia and me.

"I didn't sleep at all last night, although that could've been the flashing lights from the police cars. What was that about, do you know?"

I shake my head. "I'm afraid to find out. I didn't hear any gunshots or anything. Did you?"

"Nope, I heard nothing. Do you suppose the police will knock on our doors, asking us? It'll be like we're in the middle of one of the shows that film here."

I laugh, but she's right. Often, we'd have to reroute ourselves on our way home from work because of filming. I thought about signing up to be an extra, thinking it would've been fun, but never did. There's still time if I come back.

"If they're going to ask, they better do so quickly. What time is your flight tomorrow?"

"It's not until nine a.m. Want to grab dinner tonight? For old time's sake?"

"I'd love to, but I can't. I'm taking the eight-fifteen out of JFK to head home."

Talia masks her disappointment with a forced smile. "You probably have lots to do, right?"

I nod. "Classes start back up on Monday."

"Thankfully, I have a week off."

"Lucky. Right back to the grind. I can already feel senioritis setting in. Living close to the beach isn't going to help."

"What's it like?" she asks. I'm on the cusp of telling her she should visit, but don't want to send the wrong message. Everyone is free to come to California.

However, I don't want her to think I'm inviting her to stay with me. I know it's a hard assumption to make.

"It's amazing. It's always sunny and warm, and the sky is always blue. Granted, we do have crappy weather from time to time, but nothing like New York. We can go to the beach almost all year round. My friends and I surf a lot."

"Sounds like heaven. I've been landlocked my entire life until I came out here. Being near the water, albeit a gross infested river, was nice. I'm going to miss it. And you," she says.

"I'll miss you too, Talia. Thank you for being such an amazing co-worker."

There's an awkward silence between us, where we're just looking at each other. We both jump when my intercom goes off, and Margie's assistant is requesting we meet the managers in the boardroom.

"Here we go," I say, motioning her to walk in front of me. When we arrive, the other four are filing into the room in front of us.

Roy looks confident, while Ashley looks like she's on the verge of tears. Tara is picking at her nails, and Jeff is fidgeting with his jacket, buttoning and unbuttoning it repeatedly. I want to set my hand on top of his to still his movements, but I don't. Instead, I stand behind Talia and wait for the outcome.

"Good morning," Margie's boss says. "We won't keep you long as we're all aware you have some packing to take care of and flights to catch." He looks at the six of us and smiles. "When Omni started the internship, the length was six months long, and we saw students waiting until the last minute to get their projects done. When we switched it to three months, productivity increased tenfold, giving us a better opportunity to assess the finest six applicants of the current graduating class. With that said, the Board is pleased with the outcome of your work. Each team has given their manager fresh new ideas to take our clients' needs to the next level. However, this is a competition, with the winning team receiving an employment offer."

"Congratulations, Tara and Roy." We clap, even if it's half-hearted. I wanted to win, more so for Talia. Margie's boss goes on to say a few more things, but I've since tuned him out.

Talia and I walk back to our cubicle. She's somber, and I don't blame her. I pretend to be, but it's hard knowing I have a job waiting for me. "I'm going to go," I tell her. "I have a few things to do before my flight."

"Goodbye, Ben. If you're ever in Iowa, look me up." I hug her before leaving and don't tell her the same thing. She has my number, and if she uses it if she finds herself in Los Angeles, great. Although, I don't think Elle would like it too much.

The truth is, I have nothing to do, except go to the airport. I've been packed for the last couple of days and living out of my suitcase. As soon as I'm free of the building, I pull out my phone to call Elle.

"Hey," she says, answering immediately. "Did you win?"

"Nope, we lost, but I'm okay with it. Just sad for Talia."

"So now what?"

"Now, I'm going to wait at the airport and see if I can get on the standby list to fly home early."

"Okay, keep me updated. I have to run to class."

"Will do." I can't wait to tell her that I love her again, but not over the phone. I want to look her in the eyes and say the words so she knows I mean them.

I only have to wait on standby for a few flights before I'm finally on a plane and heading back to Los Angeles. Elle promises to be at the airport, which pisses off my brother. He doesn't understand how I can forgive her so easily. It's easy; I'm in love. For most of the flight I sleep, and when I'm not sleeping, I'm scrolling through the pictures on my phone.

The second my plane touches down, I'm antsy, eager to get out of my seat and find Elle waiting for me at baggage claim. Before I even booked my flight, Elle said I could use the private jet, but I didn't want to seem like I was taking advantage of her or the band. Now I wish I did because the wait is killing me.

I'm in a full sprint, weaving in and out of people with my backpack slapping against my ass, which is somewhat annoying.

When I enter baggage claim, I stop dead in my tracks. There's my beautiful girlfriend standing there holding a sign with my name on it. I go to her and scoop her up into my arms and twirl her around. "I've missed you so much," I tell her. There's nothing like starting a relationship, and not being able to see each other when you want. Face-Time doesn't cut it.

"I've missed you too," she says as I put her down. Elle

continues to hold my face and looks into my eyes. "I have something to tell you."

"Can it wait until we're home?" I ask. There are too many people in the airport right now, and I'd much prefer she tell me in private.

Elle shakes her head. "No, it can't."

"Okay, what is it?" My hands tighten around her waist, giving me a bit of security.

"I love you, Benjamin. It's taken me a long time to realize this, but now that I have, there's no stopping it. You're my unexpected love, one I never thought I'd find, at least not in my best friend."

I lean down and kiss her. I've waited most of my life to hear those words from her, and we could be in a completely different situation had I had the courage to say them years ago. For all I know, we'd have been together, but we could also be apart, living life as former friends.

Elle doesn't take me back to our apartment complex but drives to her parents. I have to say I'm not exactly looking forward to spending time with Mr. and Mrs. PJ when I'd rather be alone with Elle, but I don't question her. It's late, and she's definitely up to something because each time I ask her what's going on, she clams up.

Because of the time change, I'm tired and rest my eyes while she drives us south. Had I known she wanted to come this way, I would've flown into a different airport. When her Wrangler slows down, I open my eyes, only I don't recognize where we are.

"Elle?"

"Hey, sleepyhead."

"Where are we?" I yawn and start stretching my cramped muscles.

"Malibu. I rented a house for the weekend."

"You did?"

She nods. "I thought we could use some time to ourselves without Quinn hanging around."

The console between keeps us separated, but I still manage to pull her into a kiss. "This is perfect. Come on there's something we need to do."

"What's that?" she asks as she gets out of her car. I rush around to the other side and pick her up. She squeals, making me laugh.

Once we're at the door, I put her down so she can unlock it. Inside, the house is white and gray, with massive floor to ceiling windows that look out over the ocean. Tomorrow, the view's going to be spectacular once the sun rises.

Elle takes my hand and leads me down the hall to the bedroom. She steps in first and holds the door, while I take in the surroundings. There are rose petals on the bed, floor, and furniture with what I'm hoping are battery operated candles burning, giving off a romantic ambiance.

"Elle?" I reach for her and press my lips together. "Are you sure?"

"I have never been surer."

31

ELLE

*I*t took me a few days to find this house, but once I did, I didn't hesitate to book it. The only problem is, I had to do it for a month, and with school starting its final quarter, there's no way Ben and I can stay here for that amount of time. However, I wanted to do something special for him when he came back, more so, something special for us.

Keeping this secret from Ben has been hard. We promised to tell each other everything, and I like to think he'll forgive me once he wakes up and sees the view from the bedroom. While we may not be able to stay all week, we can come back Thursday night and stay until Sunday. I'm excited that neither of us has classes on Friday.

Ben snuggles into my back, and this time when he kisses my bare shoulder, I don't flinch or recoil. I relish in his touch, the softness of his hands and the tender way he's spent the night making love to me. I know we were supposed to wait, but I couldn't. Once I left New York, my heart hurt more than it ever had. There's no question in my mind that I want to be with Ben, now and forever. Together, he and I are going to be super cheesy, corny and probably argue a lot because we're both stubborn, but it's going to be worth it.

"So beautiful," he says as his lips ghost along the top of my shoulder, peppering me with his kisses.

"I know it is." To think we're going to give this up… it's the right thing to do for Ben's career. My job's going to be mobile. I can do it from anywhere as long as there's a band playing.

"I'm talking about you." He stops, allowing me to turn over. My hand immediately goes to his chest so I can feel his heart beating.

"You haven't even seen the view," I tell him.

"I don't need to, not when I have you to look at."

I bury my face in his chest, feeling embarrassed. He laughs, the reverberations shaking the bed. "Get used to it, Elle. I'm going to compliment you all the time." It's not that I've never been complimented, it's that when most guys did it, it's because they wanted something I wasn't willing to give. However, when Ben does it, it's different. There's so much sincerity behind his words, love in his eyes and tenderness in his touch, I know he means it every time he says something kind.

"What do you want to do today? We can go surfing," I tell him.

"I have a better idea," Ben says as he starts kissing me. His hand slides under my leg, lifting it over his hip. I can feel him at my entrance, poised and ready, all I have to do is push my hips into him. I do, not caring whether he's using a condom or not. He's my Ben, and he'll never do anything to hurt me.

By lunchtime, my stomach is growling. We haven't left the bed, other than to drink some water and use the restroom. Oh, and shower because Ben said we needed to take advantage of the dual showerheads.

"You're right," Ben says while standing in front of the window.

"About what?" I walk over to him with a sandwich. The view is stunning. It astounds me.

"This view. It's hard to give it up."

I place my hand on his shoulder and kiss him there. "I'm sure the east coast is pretty in its own way."

He shakes his head. "I've been thinking, maybe Omni isn't the right fit for me."

"Why do you say that?" I ask.

"Because I love it here. I love the sun, the weather. I love to surf. I'm not sure New York offers us the life we want."

"And what do you want, Ben?"

Ben sets his plate down and pulls me into his arms. "I want us, Elle. And I know you've said you'll move. Hell, you did that before I even could ask you, which meant the world to me, but look at our lives. We spend so much of our free time at the beach. We love it here. Why should we give it up?"

"Because we're adults now," I tell him. "Or at least we will be in a few short months."

"I know, but..." He shakes his head.

I place my hands on each side of his face so he'll look directly at me and not be caught off guard by the ocean. "What's going on? I thought Omni was your dream."

"It still is."

"So what gives?"

He points toward the beach. "What if this is my dream too and I didn't realize it until now. What if I'm making a mistake? What if we get there and we hate it, or you start to hate me?"

"Moving comes with risks."

"Not when you don't need to take them," he says. "There are plenty of firms here I could work for, plus Brad's here. I could go out on my own and start my own company, or you and I could band together, and create an agency that offers everything."

As soon as Ben says that, my eyes light up. "Are you serious about the last part?"

He nods. "I am. I've thought about it before, but never thought to bring it up. Think about it, baby. If you manage the talent side and I do their marketing, they wouldn't need multiple people working for them."

"That could be an enticing offer to someone starting out. I think you're onto something, Mr. Miller."

"The only thing I want to be on right now is you Miss Powell-James." Ben picks me and runs down the hall to the bedroom, where he sets me down on the bed.

"Can I ask you a serious question, which will probably freak you out?"

"Sure," I say, as I start to take off my robe. Ben closes his eyes for reasons unknown, but if I had to guess, it's so he can concentrate on his question and not my nakedness.

"When we're married because let's face it, it's going to happen, are you going to hyphenate your name?"

I laugh, and while the thought of marriage weeks into a relationship should scare me, it doesn't. "You mean so I can be Elle Powell-James-Miller?"

"Such a mouthful."

"I know. Professionally, Elle James." I beckon Ben with my finger as I shimmy my way up the mattress. He follows, crawling toward me like a cat does its prey. "However, when we're not working, I'd really like to be Mrs. Miller."

"Yeah, I like that."

"I thought you would, Mr. Miller."

"I'm going to love you forever."

"Yeah, I like that," I tell him, using the same words he just said.

This is how Ben and I spend our first weekend together, tangled in the sheets while life moves on around us. We're not naïve to think everything's going to be easy. Two people just out of college and starting their own business is going to be hard, but we're both confident in our abilities to make sure we succeed and that the talent who entrusts us are successful.

Now that our future is somewhat planned out, we have to move onto bigger, more important things, like... Peyton's wedding and finding Quinn a date! And given the wedding will be on us sooner than we think, Quinn's love life definitely takes priority.

ACKNOWLEDGMENTS

Many thanks to those who helped with this story: Amy & Amber thank you for pre-reading and providing feedback. Thank you, Sarah, for another amazing cover. And Ellie: thank you for dropping everything to editing. Ena & Amanda, thank you! I really appreciate all your help. Drue & Debra, you've changed so much for me in the past year, thank you!

Yvette, I don't know how many times I can tell you thank you, but thank you! Your hard work never goes unnoticed.

To my street team, thank you for making sure my teasers are everywhere.

Ashley, you may be my sister, but having you help me on a daily basis has been a blessing. Thank you!

To all the readers, writing Elle wasn't easy. The road to redemption is a hard one, and I hope I've done her justice.

ABOUT HEIDI MCLAUGHLIN

Heidi McLaughlin is a New York Times, Wall Street Journal, and USA Today Bestselling author of The Beaumont Series, The Boys of Summer, and The Archers.

Originally, from the Pacific Northwest, she now lives in picturesque Vermont, with her husband, two daughters, and their three dogs.

In 2012, Heidi turned her passion for reading into a full-fledged literary career, writing over twenty novels, including the acclaimed Forever My Girl.

When writing isn't occupying her time, you can find her sitting courtside at either of her daughters' basketball games.

Heidi's first novel, Forever My Girl, has been adapted into a motion picture with LD Entertainment and Roadside Attractions, starring Alex Roe and Jessica Rothe, and opened in theaters on January 19, 2018.

Don't miss more books by Heidi McLaughlin! Sign up for her newsletter, or join the fun in her fan group!

Connect with Heidi!
www.heidimclaughlin.com

ALSO BY HEIDI MCLAUGHLIN

THE BEAUMONT SERIES

Forever My Girl – Beaumont Series #1

My Everything – Beaumont Series #1.5

My Unexpected Forever – Beaumont Series #2

Finding My Forever – Beaumont Series #3

Finding My Way – Beaumont Series #4

12 Days of Forever – Beaumont Series #4.5

My Kind of Forever – Beaumont Series #5

Forever Our Boys - Beaumont Series #5.5

The Beaumont Boxed Set - #1

THE BEAUMONT SERIES: NEXT GENERATION

Holding Onto Forever

My Unexpected Love

THE ARCHER BROTHERS

Here with Me

Choose Me

Save Me

LOST IN YOU SERIES

Lost in You

Lost in Us

THE BOYS OF SUMMER

Third Base

Home Run

Grand Slam

THE REALITY DUET

Blind Reality

Twisted Reality

SOCIETY X

Dark Room

Viewing Room

Play Room

THE CLUTCH SERIES

Roman

STANDALONE NOVELS

Stripped Bare

Blow

Sexcation

Santa's Secret

HOLDING
ONTO
FOREVER

THE BEAUMONT SERIES - NEXT GENERATION

Kyle Zimmerman, one of the top-rated quarterbacks in the league, and Chicago's most eligible bachelor is holding my hand as he guides me to his car. The school-girl in me is trying not to let his presence affect me, at least not on the outside. On the inside, though, I'm all a ball of nerves mixed with excitement. Who would've thought a simple assignment would turn into a date? Not me. Not in a million years, but here I am, being helped into his car and anxiously waiting for him to get behind the steering wheel.

And once he does, the sweet scent of his cologne fills the small space. I find myself leaning a bit closer to him so I can inhale deeply without looking like a creeper. Kyle smiles. It's an ear-to-ear grin with a slight chuckle. I've been caught, but he doesn't seem to care. He leans forward, pulling himself away from me. It's probably best. We've just met and if he kissed me now, I don't know what I would do.

"Tell me about yourself, Peyton."

"I'm majoring in broadcast journalism. I love football. I'm a twin."

"Is your twin as pretty as you?"

"Prettier," I tell him.

"Impossible," he replies, never breaking eye contact with me. "What do you know about me?"

"Everything, yet nothing. Your rookie year, you sat on the bench but started your second year. You threw sixteen touchdowns, eleven interceptions and accumulated 3,440 yards. Your completion rate was fifty-eight percent. This year, you're pushing seventy percent and in line to win the league MVP. You've thrown for almost 4,500 yards, twenty-five touchdowns and four interceptions."

Kyle's eyes widen as his mouth drops open. "Wow, you had to go and bring up my first year, huh?"

I shrug. "You asked, but ..."

"But what?" he asks, adjusting the way he's sitting.

I run my cold hands down my pant legs to create some heat. "I don't know anything personal about you, aside from your age, where you were born, etc.... all stuff that is easily found on the internet. I'd like to get to know the real you."

"You're right, so what do you say we head to dinner and talk about who we are away from football?"

"I'd like that."

Kyle starts his car and pulls out of the parking lot.

There's very minimal traffic waiting to get out the exit the players use.

"Tell me, Peyton. How do you know so much about football?"

"Well, my dad and best friend..."

"Ms. Powell-James, I'd like to see you after class," *Professor Fowler says, calling me out in front of everyone. An email would've sufficed if he needed to see me after class. As is, all the males in class all make comments on how I'm in trouble, and the few other females sneer at me. Who knew journalism is so cutthroat? I sling my backpack over my shoulder and take the steps down to where my professor is standing.*

"You wanted to see me, sir?" I close my eyes at the idiocy of my statement. Of course he wanted to see me, he called me down, humiliating me in front of the entire class.

"Peyton, you're one of my best students."

"Thank you."

"Your knowledge of sports, particularly football will get you far."

"I owe it all to the men in my family." If it weren't for my father introducing me to the sport and Liam coming into my life when he did, I could've easily fallen out of love with it. Noah was there, of course, but I could've become a cheerleader or not had anything to do with the game entirely.

"Well, make sure you tell your family that you'll be on the sidelines for this week's Bears game." The professor hands me a lanyard with the word Media *written all over it. Attached to the clip is a press pass with my name on it.*

"I don't understand."

"It's simple. This Sunday, you'll be representing the school and me at the game. I expect a full write-up of the game on my desk on Monday morning. Everything you need to know will be emailed to you later this evening. You've earned this, Peyton. Enjoy it."

"But why me?"

"Because you're the best." He picks up his briefcase and exits through the faculty door, leaving me in the room staring at what is surely going to be my most prized possession until I become an official member of the media. I slip it around my neck and hide it under my scarf, hiding it from anyone who may be lingering out in the hall.

As soon as I push the heavy door open, I spot a group of my classmates. With my head down, I rush by them, praying none of them say anything.

"Hold up, Peyton." The voice belongs to Donnie Olson, the self-proclaimed God of all things sports. He thinks because he knows more about rugby and soccer, he's the king.

"Hey, Donnie."

"What did Fowler want?"

"To ask about my friend."

"Right. I forgot you're 'best friends' with Noah Westbury."

I don't stop when he mocks me. I made the mistake of telling a sorority sister about Noah. She didn't believe me, going as far as saying Noah going to prom with me was a charity fundraiser I won. And it's not like I've been able to prove her otherwise since he's been dating Dessie, which has strained our relationship by no fault of his.

"Yeah, something like that." I continue to walk across campus with him right next to me. He continues to gab about Noah and Dessie, reminding me, very painfully I might add, that he's with her and how they're all over the place, with her talking about marriage. I want to plug my ears and throw up at the same time.

"Would you look at this?" I say, pointing to my sorority house. "Gotta go!" I hurry into the house and shut the door.

"Donnie, again?" Veronica, one of my sisters, asks.

I nod and head toward the stairs. "It's relentless."

"He probably wants to ask you out."

I grimace at the thought. Something about him creeps me out. I head toward my room and strip off my winter gear. I find myself standing in my mirror with my credentials hanging down. I can't help the smile that spreads across my face. Pulling out my phone, I scroll until I find Noah's name. My thumb hovers, but I don't press. I haven't called him in so long I honestly don't know what I'd say if he answered... or if she did.

Instead, I scroll up to Liam's name and call him.

"Uncle Liam, I have news." I proceed to tell him, thanking him repeatedly for helping me get to this place in my life. He tells me he'll be at Noah's game, but will try to watch the Bears game as well, hoping to see me on the sidelines. My next call is to my parents. My mom's excited, and my dad is reserved. He's never really grasped my love of football but has always encouraged me to follow my passion.

The rest of the week I'm a mess, studying not only for my classes, but the stats for the upcoming game. I focus *heavily on the Bears, but also their opponent, the Bengals. On paper, which means nothing on Sunday, the Bengals are favored to win. Still, I take my notes, jotting down things I need to watch for.*

Sleep evades me, and by the time my alarm goes off Sunday morning, I'm a zombie. I down coffee, shower, drink more coffee, do my hair and get dressed before downing yet another cup while I'm on the phone with my mother, who is basking in the warm temperatures of the Bahamas with my aunts.

Arriving early with my press credentials hanging happily around my neck, I am downright giddy and loving every second of lifting the badge to show security that I'm allowed onto the field. Walking through the tunnel, I take it all in. While the noise level is high now, it will be thunderous when kick-off happens. People start to fill the seats, while many young kids are hanging over the railings trying to grab a player or two for an autograph. The smell of popcorn and hot dogs fill the air.

And the reason I'm here... the media outlets are setting up on every corner. Microphones are being tested, makeup done so they look perfect when they're on air. This is what I want. I turn at the sounds of applause and find the Bears coming out of the tunnel. They slap the hands of their littlest fans as they go by.

Being here early has its perks, at least it does for me since I'm the newbie. I'm the one learning. An NFL field is vastly different from high school or college and the last thing I want is to find myself tripping over some random piece of equipment or find myself standing in the wrong spot. I want to know my place on the field before someone yells at me.

As the Bears warm-up, I start taking notes, writing down everything from what stretches they're doing to how many are running full sprints. None of this is important for my article, but it keeps my mind busy and keeps me from gawking at the quarterback, Kyle Zimmerman. Each time I look at the field, his eyes are on me. The first time I noticed, I smiled and quickly went back to my notepad, but now I can feel his eyes burning into me.

"Watch out," I hear, looking up in time to sidestep an errant pass made by Kyle, who is rushing toward me. I pick the pigskin up and throw it back to him, with a perfect spiral I might add.

"Whoa, on target and everything," he says with a smile so wide that his eyes appear to be twinkling. "Sorry about that, sometimes the ball just gets away from me."

"You're the quarterback. It's your job to make sure the ball hits your mark each and every time. The ball should never get away from you. You should command it to do your work for you."

He smiles and pushes his hand through his hair. There's a bit of laughter coming from him as well, which in turn makes me smile, but I try to hide it. I know football, better than most, thanks to Noah.

"I've just been schooled by a reporter," he says, shaking his head.

"Not exactly."

"What do you mean?" he asks.

"I'm a broadcast journalism major at Northwestern, but football is my life."

His smile gets wider. "Let me get this straight, not only do you understand the game, but you can throw a wicked spiral?"

I shrug as if it's no big deal.

"I think I've died and gone to heaven." The thought that Kyle Zimmerman is impressed with me sends my heartbeat into a tailspin. He places his hand over his heart and bows. I could easily say I'm following right behind him with his dark hair and five o'clock shadow. I haven't dated much since I moved to Evanston. In fact, dating in high school rarely happened either. Most of the guys always thought that Noah and I had a thing, and while there was a time in my life that I wanted us to be, we're nothing more than best friends or at least we were.

"Have dinner with me after the game? Win or lose, you and I go out and enjoy each other's company."

"We barely know each other."

Kyle steps closer. He smells like man mixed with sweat. "I'm Kyle," he says.

"I'm Peyton." His much larger hand engulfs mine, covering it completely.

"Peyton as in Manning?"

"As in Powell-James, but if you're asking if my father was a Peyton Manning fan, the answer is yes." He wasn't exactly, but when Elle and I were born, Peyton Manning was one of the best quarterbacks in the league and his brother Eli was a rookie. I think for my father, being saddled with twin girls, he wanted to do something to compensate for being the only man in the house. I never asked my mom why she allowed our father to name us after the Mannings... probably because I know it still hurts *her sometimes to talk about him. Even though she loves my dad Harrison, I know she misses my father, Mason.*

"I like it," he says, winking. "I gotta go to work." He motions toward the field with his head and that's when I make the mistake of looking. His teammates are standing there, gawking at us, with a few of them trying to hide their laughter behind their hands. If they had their jerseys on, I'd make a note of who they were so I could be sure to mention any screw-ups they had during the game. Luckily for them, I'm not a Bears fan and I don't have their roster memorized.

I try not to watch as Kyle runs back toward the rest of the team, and when he looks at me over his shoulder, I can feel my cheeks turning red. Of course, it could be because the wind is blowing and it's cold despite the sun being out or it's because I like that he's taken an interest in me.

And I really like that he's taken an interest in me.

While Kyle's car is small, he's leaning toward me, listening to everything I have to say. We haven't even left the parking lot yet, and his hand has moved closer and every few seconds I can feel his finger brush against my knuckles.

"I'm kicking myself for not throwing the ball at you until today."

I want to roast him for admitting that he was trying to hit me, but I let it go. "Today was your only opportunity. I was on an assignment. This was my first Bears game."

"And we lost."

I shrug and keep my eyes on him as he inches us forward.

"What are you in the mood for?" he asks as he brings

his car to a stop to let traffic go by, turning his head left, then right and when he looks at me, he winks.

"Someplace quiet, where we can talk."

Kyle smiles before pulling out onto the road. I barely recognize the sound of a truck horn blaring and tires screeching before I look out my window and see the word MAC heading straight toward me. As the grill of the truck smashes into my side of the car, I raise my hand to protect my face from the flying glass and I wonder if this was what my father did all those years ago when he met the eighteen-wheeler that took his life.

r o m a n

New York Times and *USA Today* Bestselling Author

HEIDI MCLAUGHLIN
AND AMY BRIGGS

Lights flash, like an eternal disco, lighting up the night sky. Nobody visiting keeps time in Las Vegas, the true city that never sleeps. Faces race by slowly, my heightened vision enabling me to make out every feature, from a crooked nose to fake eyelashes. Tourists from all over the world flock to the desert. Some to vacation in the sun, some hoping for their big break, others desperate for a fresh start. Everyone needs a change of pace or something different every now and again, even myself.

The humidity from the building, the people, and the general metropolis Las Vegas has become, traps the heat on the Strip. I prefer the area just outside of the city, where the desert is cooler, where the sun retreats behind the mountains in the distance, and the crisp air is free of the city pollution. Each night, as the sun begins to tuck itself into bed, the pink reflection left on the mountainside is meditative. I try to catch the sunset every evening, as it has brought a calm and peaceful appreciation for my surroundings. When you've lived as long as I have, finding moments of serenity are a rare gift.

My impatience grows as I continue to wait for

Melody with whom I had an appointment twenty minutes ago. Humans are always late and full of selfish excuses for it. When she arrives, her face is flushed, and her chest is heaving slightly as she catches her breath.

"Roman. I am so sorry I'm late."

"I was beginning to wonder if you changed your mind about working with me." She hasn't, I can tell by the racing of her heart. She's nervous, not because of what I am, but out of the fear that I'll dismiss her. She knows a big commission when she sees one. To me from the moment we met was evident, and if I didn't have more specific standards in consorts, I might have taken her up on her advances, as she was easy prey.

"You know you're my favorite client." Her head tilts to the left, showing me her jugular. My tongue darts out, passing over my razor-sharp teeth. Melody doesn't wear a cross, meaning she'd be perfectly comfortable if I were to compel her, but I refrain. Not because I'm in public, but more so because I'm trying to keep business away from pleasure. However, allowing Melody to think she has a chance is no exception. Pleasure always seems to win out in the end.

Over the years, the ability to pick up and play off of human weaknesses has become second nature. "Yes, well, then let's get down to business, shall we?" The casino property that I want to purchase has just gone on the market. The current owners had no idea what they were getting into when they bought it. Renovations and upkeep to accommodate millions of people running through the doors of casinos require significant work and operational management. It's not as simple as putting your name on the deed and collecting the cash that rolls in.

"Of course. Again, I'm so sorry I'm late." She reaches into her bag and pulls out a large blue folder with her company's logo on the front, and hands it to me. "Here is the prospectus for the property. A full view of everything top to bottom. Would you like to look at them over a drink?" She smiles, with a hopeful look in her eyes.

"I believe you already know I don't drink." I smirk at her, acknowledging her proposition. I had to give her an A for effort. She didn't lay it on too thick but made her intentions known nonetheless.

"That's right, I almost forgot." She grins, shrugging her shoulders.

"Let's walk around the place again so that I can be sure I know what I need to before filing the formal papers." I tuck the folder under my arm, not reviewing it. I've already seen the blueprints of the property; in fact, I have them memorized. I know exactly what I'm getting into. However, achieving a certain level of comfort with the people I have to do business with is of the utmost importance. The only questions I have remaining are ensuring I file the necessary paperwork with the municipality and the gaming commission.

We walk silently around the exterior of the building before going inside to talk. Melody picks at the skin on her thumb nervously, waiting for me to speak once we sit down at a bar table inside the casino.

"Are you nervous around me, Melody?" I ask sardonically.

Dropping her hands to her lap, she shakes her head.

"No, Roman. Not at all. I mean I've never done business with a vampire before, but it's no big deal. Just like doing business with anyone else. I think you are all great." She rambles.

"You can relax Melody. You do know that we don't go around biting people whenever we want. That is unless we're invited of course," I reply smoothly. I'm flirting back, and while I have no interest in feeding off her, or fucking her for that matter, it's a behavior that is instinctive. Vampires by nature are virile. It's a glorious affliction to be attractive to the opposite sex and to have the ability to pick and choose, which wasn't always the case. For many years we hid, unable to walk among the humans as we do now. They hunted us, killing off the population because of who we are.

"Oh, I know." She grins, shifting in her seat. "My friend says you only bite people who want to be bitten."

"Your friend is correct." My eyes shift, watching her turn her engagement ring around her finger until I force myself to focus on the issue at hand, buying the casino. "So, Melody, I'm in. I want you to broker this deal. I'd like to expedite this process though as quickly as possible. I have plans to renovate immediately, and subsequently, I have plans to construct an additional unrelated building with the net gains from this property. So, the contract needs to include not only this casino but the empty lot that we discussed outside of downtown as well. Can you handle this?"

"Of course I can. Have you filed the necessary permits with the gaming commission or the township?"

"Yes and no. My permits to renovate are filed;

however, I'm unclear exactly what needs to be done with the gaming commission. Doesn't the property come with the license?" I've tried looking into this, but the information provided on the commission's website is archaic at best, and that says a lot, coming from a five hundred-year-old vampire.

"I was afraid of that." She purses her lips thoughtfully as if she has more to add.

"What is it?" I demand.

"You have to file for your own gaming license. There's a set number available, and yours will be the one that's given up by the current owners. But, there's a bit of a snag we haven't discussed yet." The ring twisting has stopped, and she looks at me with pure fear in her eyes. Not responding, I raise my eyebrows at her, and gently spin my hand for her to continue.

"Well, the head of the gaming commission... he's a difficult man. And, as it turns out, he doesn't like to do business with vampires. As in, he won't give you a license. But, not to worry. Now, what I suggest you do, is find yourself a human who you can trust, and have them file the paperwork to get the license," she explains hesitantly.

"So, you're saying I can't actually own my own casino? I have to get a business partner, which I do not want, by the way, to act as my surrogate so that I can get this piece of paper?"

"Unless you can come up with a way to warm him up to vampires, then yes. That is exactly what I'm saying. I realize you weren't looking for a partnership, but in this town, the gaming commissioner is the head honcho.

They... well he, controls everything. And Mr. Weston is quite known for his anti-vampire stance."

"Mr. Weston," I repeat quietly. Going straight to the sore spot on a sensitive subject such as this seems irresponsible. It took hundreds of years for vampires to be able to walk about freely, openly as vampires, and for the holdouts to the cause, it was never a good idea to become confrontational. This is going to take some degree of finesse.

"Yes, Mr. James Weston. He is who you're going to need approval from. All gaming licenses require his signature. Once you have that, we can move forward with the deal. But, until then, I can keep it pending under contract, so another buyer doesn't swoop in."

I lean forward, placing my palms on top of Melody's hands. As she meets my gaze, I whisper, "You will make sure that no one else gets this property, right Melody?"

Under my compulsion, her eyes glaze over as she nods slowly. "I will make sure no one else gets this property."

"Thank you, Melody."

"Of course, Roman," she mutters quietly, still under my artificial rapture.

"I will be in touch." I stand up, grasping the folder with the blueprints and plans in it, and shove it back under my arm. I repeat the name of the obstacle in my way over and over as I make my way toward the exit. I need to find a way to turn this Mr. Weston into an ally, instead of a vampire fearing foe. As I walk out of the casino, the various voices around me are a stark reminder that humans are vain. Each one has a price, a weakness of some kind, a social ladder they need to climb, and when someone with my power, resources, and income comes along with a proposition, they buckle at the knees, begging to do business with me. It won't take much for me to figure out how feeble Mr. Weston is. If anything, I'm more determined now than ever to buy this property. As far as I'm concerned, Mr. Weston has no idea what he's in for.